A Season
in the *Keys*

≈ A COCONUT KEY NOVEL ≈
BOOK THREE

HOPE
HOLLOWAY

A Season in the Keys

Coconut Key Book 3

Cover designed by Sarah Brown (http://www.sarahdesigns.co/)

Edited by Lorie Humpherys

INTRODUCTION TO COCONUT KEY

If you're longing for an escape to paradise, step on to the gorgeous, sun-kissed sands of Coconut Key. With a cast of unforgettable characters and stories that touch every woman's heart, these delightful novels will make you laugh out loud, fall in love, and stand up and cheer...and then you'll want the next one *right this minute*.

For release dates, excerpts, news, and more, sign up to receive Hope Holloway's newsletter! Or visit www.hopeholloway.com and follow Hope on Facebook and BookBub!

CHAPTER ONE
BECK

*B*illy Dobson. Her high school crush. The father of the baby she'd given up for adoption when she was sixteen.

Not a whole lot could throw Rebecca Foster, but greeting a man she hadn't seen for forty years as he stood in her driveway and announced that he was the contractor who would renovate her B&B? That knocked her for a loop.

Beck swallowed a second slug of mimosa, this shocking fact pressing down as hard as the August sunshine over Coquina House.

Then she turned to a very guilty-looking Kenny Gallagher, a tendril of disappointment curling around her heart as she looked at her son. Not a son she'd raised, since she'd only recently met the man she'd given up for adoption the day he was born. So, maybe *disappointment* wasn't warranted.

After all, Beck didn't expect to know everything about his life. But they had made tremendous strides these past months since his daughter, Ava, had shown up on Beck's doorstep. He'd renovated her kitchen, and they'd cobbled together their version of a reunited family.

But why didn't he tell her that he knew—obviously quite well—his biological father? He was clearly friends with the man who had signed papers forty years ago swearing he'd never seek contact with or custody of the baby.

In the doorway of Coquina House, Billy Dobson— she supposed he went by Bill now—chatted and laughed with Ava, Kenny's daughter who was responsible for all of them knowing each other in the first place. Obviously, Ava and Kenny and Bill were like family.

Not like family. They *were* family.

She called him "Uncle Bill," so Ava didn't know Bill was her grandfather...*did she?*

Beck turned to Kenny, all the questions jumbled in her brain, but only one rising to the top. "Why didn't you tell me?"

"Honestly, he asked me not to. Maybe he was worried about legal stuff, maybe he just wanted to let you have your time with us."

"But he's *here*," she said. "As a contractor."

"I told him you were searching high and low for a contractor and he's got a Florida license, so that makes sense."

Did it? Right now, nothing made sense.

Beck shifted her gaze back to Bill who lingered on the front porch talking to Ava. In the house, her family and friends were oblivious to this new drama, currently gathered on her back veranda to celebrate the fact that Beck had just signed divorce papers and ended a thirty-four-year marriage.

"Oh, brother." This time, she drained the "celebration mimosa" and gave a dry smile to Kenny. "Or should I say 'oh father and son'? How did he find you? How did he get your name as his son?"

"DNA," Kenny said. "His kids did a group DNA test and all three of them got these strange results that showed a direct sibling relation to someone they didn't know...and that someone was me."

"You did a DNA test?" she asked, surprised again by something he didn't tell her.

"My wife did one on me but never told me. The results came after she died, sent in an email to her, so if I saw that, I probably deleted it as junk mail. I really don't remember, but it was before Bill's kids did it, so their information wouldn't have been in the database then."

"Was she looking for your birth parents?" Beck asked.

"She was curious, much more than I was. Elise wondered about health and genes, that sort of thing, and my mother claimed to know nothing, although she obviously did know your name despite the 'sealed' adoption. As I've told you, as far as I was concerned, my parents were Janet and Jim Gallagher, and I never harbored some bone-deep need for a reunion."

"Did he?" she asked, tipping her head toward Bill.

"I think he did. At least, when his kids showed him that they all were likely half-siblings to someone in the database named Kenneth Gallagher, he got intrigued with the idea of meeting me. It wasn't hard to find me since he had my name and I never left Atlanta."

Beck searched his face, imagining how a meeting like that would unfold. "What happened?"

He gave a dry laugh. "He walked up to me in a coffee shop about ten minutes after I did a twenty-four-hour paramedic shift and I was wiped out." His expression softened, as if the memory affected him. "Came right out and asked me if I was adopted and...we put a few things together and, well, we look a lot alike."

They certainly did. "Do people know? His kids? Ava?"

"Nope." He shook his head. "We didn't tell anyone. But we did become friends. I met him a few months after my wife passed, and he just sort of hit me at the right time. I needed a friend and a fresh perspective on a crappy life. I wanted to dial back my hours at the fire station because it was just..." He swallowed. "Bad memories."

Of course, his wife and son died in a fire.

"So, I started working for him and he's been a great boss. And a greater friend." He slid another look at Bill, who was coming down the stairs after Ava went inside. "But this? Showing up without warning? Not really like him, to be honest."

As Bill came closer, Beck studied the man, now fifty-six like she was. Next to Kenny, the resemblance was strong. Not so strong that a stranger would note it, but she could see the similarities. She always had seen a younger Billy Dobson in Kenny's face, with his dark eyes and chin cleft, but side by side, it was hard to deny.

"Rebecca Foster." Bill gave her an easy smile and a bigger one for Kenny. "Surprise, surprise. The family is all here."

Kenny didn't seem amused. "What are you doing here?"

"You need a contractor," he said, looking at Beck. "And I need...a break. Hey, we all know the truth now, so..."

"Ava doesn't," Kenny said, his voice strained. "And I'm on the fence about telling her now that she's really getting her act together. Everything's changed with her, I told you that."

"We don't have to tell her," Bill said, a shrug of his broad shoulders that showed he somehow was still that weirdly cool kid he'd been forty years ago. Nothing fazed him then or now. "I can just be your contractor."

"And we're not telling anyone else?" Beck asked. "My daughters or my mother, although..." Her mother knew the story, and the name of Kenny's father.

"Your mother is here?" Now Bill looked a little horrified. "'Cause that woman still haunts my nightmares."

She bit back a laugh because Olivia Mitchell could have that effect on a person, especially the teenage boy who'd knocked up her daughter. "Well, just to complicate things further..."

"Yeah, the family tree's a little gnarled," Kenny muttered.

"That woman you met when we were teenagers?" Beck said. "Olivia Mitchell? She wasn't my mother, but she raised me."

He looked rightfully confused.

"My mother was actually her much younger sister who got pregnant as a teenager and was convinced to give me to her sister to raise," Beck explained. "I only just learned that when I came down here to get to know my 'aunt'—who is named Lovely. She's my partner on the B&B we're opening here."

The frown of confusion softened as he bit back a bemused laugh. "Well, quite a churned-up gene pool we've got here."

"We've smoothed out the waters," Beck assured him. "Until you showed up."

"Causing whitewater," he laughed. "Sorry. But I know you need a contractor, and I am at your service."

"Why?" Beck asked, feeling like the more he laughed about this, the more irritation flicked at her every nerve ending.

"Uh, you can't find anyone else?"

"I will, eventually."

"I'm the best in the business." He glanced at Kenny. "Did you tell her that?"

"I didn't mention you much."

But he had talked about his friend and boss, Bill, Beck recalled. And Ava had waxed poetically about her funny, generous, wonderful Uncle Bill, who wasn't really an uncle. And all the while, Beck had been...duped.

"I don't know," she said, shaking her head. "Things are just getting under control around here." And something about Bill Dobson felt...out of control. Like those ancient, girly feelings she once had for him. Could they rear their ugly head forty years later?

She *had* ogled him when she came around the corner and saw the handsome silver-haired man inspecting her property. That would have to stop, stat.

"What's to know?" he asked, obviously a man who didn't believe in roadblocks. Or, if memory served her correctly, condoms. "Look, I'll help you get started. File the permits, work up some plans. I got a buddy in Key West who's a residential architect, perfect for this job. He's really into keeping the history and vibe of a place like this. I'll hire the trades, put Kenny in charge of everything, and leave. How's that sound?"

If he weren't precisely who he was, it would sound great. Like music to Beck's contractor-less ears. But...

"What do we tell people?" Kenny asked, putting Beck's thoughts into words. "And by people, I mean Ava."

Bill flinched a little, the very first sign of any kind of weakness that Beck had seen.

"I'd cut off my arm before I hurt that kid," he said softly. "Why should anything change? I came down to do you a favor, like friends do. Does anyone around here know the name of this guy's biological father?" He put a hand on Kenny's shoulder. "Can we keep it a secret?"

"My mother, Lovely, knows your name. But if anyone can keep a secret, it's Lovely Ames."

Bill gave a questioning look to Kenny. "You're the father, here. This is your call. Last time we talked about it, you wanted to tell her."

"I know. But I haven't seen her this happy and free of panic attacks in years. I'm really on the fence."

"Entirely your decision, son." He angled his head in deference to Beck. "Respect to you, ma'am, but Kenny's got to make this call."

Beck blinked at him. Did he just *ma'am* her? Like he was younger than she was? Ooh, he was going to get under her skin. But...he did offer a great solution to a massive problem. And create more.

"Let's just sit on it for a while," Kenny said. "She's doing well and I don't want to rock her world."

Beck wasn't at all sure she agreed with that. She knew from experience that one lie leads to more lies and more lies lead to heartbreaking and life-changing revelations. But Bill was right. This was Kenny's call.

"So, let's not tell her," Kenny said. "Bill is just a family friend who came to help us out of a bind. That's exactly who he is. The fact that he...and you..."

Bill winked at her. "We did."

She cut him with a look that only made him laugh.

"Well, Beck, come on."

"If you're going to make jokes about some...some wild night in a car forty years ago, then—"

"A car?" Kenny choked.

"A *car*?" Bill also choked. "A gold 1979 Camaro Berlinetta, which is so much more than a car. With a very tight but adequate back seat, if I recall correctly."

"Nobody wants to hear that," Kenny said.

"Including me," Beck added.

"Okay, okay. But it was the ultimate ride." Bill gave Beck a sly smile that just sent irritation scampering up her spine.

"So, show me this B&B." He turned toward the house. "Is this it? 'Cause it's stinkin' gorgeous. Who built this beauty right smack dab on the Atlantic Ocean?" He stared at the house, his dark gaze sliding over each window and detail like it was a beautiful woman he wanted to undress.

Oh, Beck. *You can't go there. You cannot go there.*

"Wait till you see the place, Bill," Kenny said, putting a hand on Bill's shoulder and guiding him to the house. "It's beachy and a little Victorian, and you're gonna cry when you see the kitchen I just finished."

"I think it was the pictures you sent that got me here," Bill said as they walked, then he slowed his step and turned to Beck as Kenny continued toward the stairs. "There was one of you," he added.

She just stared at him, determined to show absolutely no reaction to that.

"You look good, Beck. You'd never know forty years have passed."

"Thanks."

"And do you always walk around with empty champagne glasses?" He dinged her empty flute with a finger, looking more troubled than amused by that.

"Oh..." She glanced at the long-gone mimosa. "We were celebrating."

"The new kitchen?" he asked.

"My, um...divorce," she said, suddenly feeling ridiculous and self-conscious. "I just signed the papers."

His dark brows flicked up. "Well, I'd say congratulations, but I know from experience that can be a bittersweet day."

She nodded, not at all sure what to say to that. She took a step toward the house where she would surely be more comfortable than under his gaze, which was as hot and relentless as the sun.

"And don't even try to pretend," he added on a whisper, getting a look from her. "You *so* remember that Camaro."

She froze and tried the dirty look again, but he just laughed and hustled to join Kenny and go inside.

Okay. She could handle this. After all, he was an answer to her fervent prayers. Beck decided not to follow but headed to the back stairs to the veranda so she could pull Lovely aside and tell her. Because she didn't think she could handle this new arrival without a little emotional backup.

BECK WAITED until she and Lovely had taken a few steps over the shell path that led toward the beach, to make sure they were out of earshot.

"I have good news and I have bad news," Beck said quickly.

"Good first." Her mother's brows drew in a frown as she pushed back her long gray ponytail. Some remnants of pink and purple dye—*thank you, Ava*—remained in the silver strands, which somehow fit the eccentric seventy-three-year-old Beck had grown to love so deeply.

"We have a contractor," Beck announced.

"What? That's fantastic!"

Kind of. "He's supposedly the best in the business, and he's Kenny's boss, come all the way from Atlanta, with his Florida contractor's license in hand. He'll get the job done and I think, if it works out, we can meet a Christmas opening deadline for our B&B." Okay, she embellished that a bit, but he did seem confident. Even a little cocky. No, cocky, definitely.

"How could there possibly be bad news, Beckie?" Lovely's voice rose with excitement as she reached out to close her hands over Beck's arm. "This is astounding."

"I'm going to tell you something that, for the time being, no one else can know. I think you'd figure it out, anyway."

"Oh, I'm intrigued."

"You're about to be gobsmacked. He's Billy Dobson... Kenny's biological father."

Lovely's jaw nearly hit her chest as she stared at Beck. "How is that possible?"

With a quick glance to the veranda where Kenny and Bill would be any moment, Beck gave Lovely a fast recap of the last few minutes. "So, after some discussion, we all agreed we're not telling anyone that I know him."

"In the biblical sense."

She choked a mirthless laugh. "You, too, Lovely? He seems to think our, uh, high school liaison is fodder for all manner of teasing and humor. Which it is not."

Lovely just smiled. "So, another secret, huh? Is this to protect Ava? Because, based on the things she's told me, she thinks the sun rises and sets on her Uncle Bill."

"Kenny thinks she's had enough turmoil and change, and she's doing so well here in Coconut Key." Then a thought occurred to Beck, making her wrinkle her nose. "You don't think he's come down here to, I don't know, win them back? He must know that Kenny is moving here and Ava's starting at Coconut Key High in September. And that can't thrill him, since they're so close. Why else would he descend on us?"

"Why does he say?"

"He didn't, really. Just that he wanted to help a family friend."

"Well, why would you give him some other nefarious motivation?"

"Because I don't know...I'm not sure I trust him." She looked toward the house, remembering the intensity in his gaze. "He's a big personality."

"And you have a history with him," Lovely said,

patting Beck's arm as she did when she wanted to offer comfort.

"Ancient history. Don't forget he signed a paper that he'd never have contact with our child or seek custody. Obviously that's moot now, but technically, he shouldn't have contacted Kenny."

"Maybe that's why he's here," she suggested. "Maybe he knew it was inevitable that you'd someday find out Ava's 'Uncle Bill' had a last name you recognized. Maybe he wanted to meet you, to find out if you're litigious. He did break a contract."

"So did Ava's grandmother when she wrote to me and asked Ava to deliver the letter in person," Beck reminded her.

"But she's gone to heaven," Lovely reminded her. "There are no lawsuits there."

"I'm not going to sue him, for goodness sake."

"Then just relax, let him be our much-needed contractor, and trust me. Your secret is safe." She slipped an arm around Beck, always that strong and steady force that filled a need. "Now, let's go meet him and welcome him and put that man to work. Coquina House will be open for Christmas!"

"If I survive him that long."

Lovely chuckled as they walked back up the stairs, reaching the veranda at the very moment Kenny and Bill walked outside to where the small group had gathered.

"Uncle Bill, come and meet everyone!" Ava sidled up to him, gazing up with a hero worship she normally saved only for Beck's middle daughter, Savannah. "Everyone, this is my Uncle, who isn't really an uncle but Dad's boss and BFF."

The group of five stopped their chatter at the announcement, turning to the door.

"And best of all," Beck said, coming into the middle of it all, "he is a licensed Florida contractor and has agreed to handle the renovation of Coquina House into a B&B!" She might have added just a tad too much enthusiasm, but she'd never been a great liar. Not that she was lying... just omitting the big story.

But that news got a huge reaction from the small crowd.

"Let me introduce you to everyone," Beck offered, ushering Bill further out on the veranda. "This is Peyton Foster, my oldest daughter."

"Oh, you look exactly like your mother," he said with a charming smile. As Peyton and Bill shook hands, Beck willed herself to tamp down her nerves. What would Peyton say if she knew she were staring at Kenny's father?

After they exchanged hellos, Beck guided him to the chaise, where Savannah looked up with interest.

"Savannah Foster, pregnant and on bed rest," Savannah announced, lifting a hand to him. "Welcome to the crazy house."

He laughed. "Is it crazy? Looks like paradise to me. Hello, Savannah. And many congratulations on your baby."

"Thank you. Don't look for a father, we're still in the process of trying to avoid him."

The father, Beck knew, was a celebrity actor living in Los Angeles who only recently learned that the one-night stand he had this past Christmas had resulted in a baby.

Bill merely lifted his brows at Savannah's news. "That sounds...dramatic."

"It might be," Savannah said.

Beck continued the introductions, coming to Callie, her youngest, who was in town that day to give Beck the divorce papers to sign. Callie had been the one to meet Bill downstairs when he arrived and come up to tell Beck her dreams of a contractor had come true.

"And I believe you met Callie, my youngest daughter, when you first got here."

Callie extended her hand first, and no doubt gave a power squeeze that she'd been practicing since the day her father told her that every person was judged by the strength of their handshake.

"We did meet already," Bill said. "I actually thought you were here on business."

"I am."

"She lives her life on business," Savannah chimed in from the cheap seats.

"I work for Foster, Hooper & Cummings, and I was—"

"Helping your mother get divorced?" he guessed, drawing a soft breath from Beck. "She told me the reason you're all...gathered." He added a frown. "They send them to law school young these days."

"I'm twenty and an intern at my dad's firm."

He nodded and looked like he filed that piece of information somewhere, no doubt to be used for a later tease. "Good for you," he said, turning to Jessie, who stood next to Callie.

"Jessica Donovan," she said with a smile. "And we could not be happier to have a contractor for the job. So happy to meet you. And this is my brother, Joshua Cross. We're both lifelong locals, so if you need anything at all, let me know. Josh is a master woodworker."

Bill looked suitably impressed as he shook one more hand, giving Beck a moment to stand back and make an inevitable comparison of the two men.

Josh was maybe an inch shorter and not quite as broad, though every bit as strong looking. Even though Bill was only about two years younger than Josh, his hair was almost pure silver, thick and wavy. Josh only had a few gray strands in his straight brown hair, which he wore long enough to graze and cover his collar.

Next to each other, Bill looked...like a silver fox. Josh looked like steady, kind man, and one who'd become a close friend these past six months. That friendship was slowly blossoming into more. She'd told him that as soon as her divorce was final, they could figure out exactly what it could become. And now, with the ink barely dry on those divorce papers, another man had blown into Coconut Key like a storm during the heart of hurricane season...which it currently was.

Bill Dobson, oozing confidence, a sly sense of humor, and just a little too much sex appeal for Beck's liking, suddenly seemed to own the little party. It almost felt like some kind of balance had shifted and it made Beck...unsteady.

"And who is this beautiful woman?" Bill asked, taking a few steps toward the last person in the party.

Lovely gave him a slow smile, that light in her green eyes that Beck had come to recognize as her own secret sense of humor and a keen ability to correctly judge people. Thank God she knew the truth.

"Lovely Ames," she said, taking his hand. Her face, barely showing the scars from the terrible car accident she'd had almost eight months ago, beamed with warmth. "Delighted to meet our new contractor, assuming you take the job."

He lifted a brow. "Why wouldn't I? That's why I came down here."

Lovely just smiled as if to say "Is it?" but she didn't need to. Beck could see Bill's shoulders square ever so slightly, as if he knew he'd met a formidable woman. A woman who knew exactly who he was.

"And I understand you and Beck will be my clients."

"Not too demanding," Lovely assured him. "I hope."

Before he could answer, Ava bounded over next to him. "Uncle Bill, I have to take you out on the skiff. Wait until you hear what happened! I saved Savannah and her baby."

"You did?"

"And then you have to see my new high school. I can drive you there. I can drive Dad's truck. And we're moving into a house really soon." She rambled on and scooted him away.

Beck sneaked a look at her mother, who lifted her brows. "I see the resemblance to Kenny," she whispered.

"Will anyone else?" Beck asked under her breath.

"That, my sweet girl, remains to be seen."

CHAPTER TWO

SAVANNAH

*A*s the conversation escalated on the veranda, Savannah shifted from one uncomfortable position to another. Since they were all riveted on the contractor, it seemed like a good time to escape and return Nick's call, since he said he only had a quick window before he had to be on set.

She had managed to keep Nick Frye in the dark for the first six months of the pregnancy, not telling him that their wild and rash one-night stand had major consequences. But guilt and the accident that nearly cost her the baby shamed her into a confession.

After all, did an A-list celebrity currently shooting a Netflix series that was sure to be a megahit even want to know that? To her surprise, he did. After she called and told him the truth, he not only wanted to know about the baby due to arrive in less than two months, he also wanted to know more about Savannah.

So their cross-country phone calls had become daily events. He talked a lot about his role as the "Magic Man," a crime-solving magician. But, so far, he hadn't said anything about his other role...the one he wanted to take in their baby's life, if any.

Savannah frequently remembered the night she'd been on the Starbucks register—Christmas night, not to put too fine a point on her sad story. She'd been lonely and depressed, worried that she'd never get her budding photography business off the ground, and feeling sorry for herself. After all, she was a twenty-nine-year-old barista who'd had a zillion addresses since she'd left home at barely eighteen. That merited her self-pity.

They'd been on a skeleton crew of losers who had no life or family at the holidays, or not enough money to get to one without sacrificing her pride, which Savannah would have had to do to let her parents pay her way back to Atlanta for the holidays. She *should* have, though. If she'd swallowed that pride, she would have been at the very last Christmas at the Alpharetta house before Dad announced he was leaving Mom, and she would not be seven months pregnant.

That night, near closing, a tall, well-built man wearing a baseball cap and a leather jacket came in, and Savannah had hoped he was the last customer for the night. She was exhausted and had wanted to get up at sunrise and shoot some pictures at the beach for the photography portfolio she'd been building.

In fact, it had been her photographer's eye that zeroed in on the man when he ambled up to the bar. He'd ordered a cold brew reserve with the swagger of someone demanding a shot of Jack straight up instead of a trendy coffee. She'd been so keen on his facial structure, imagining how her camera would love him, that she didn't realize that he was a famous face that the camera and a whole lot of people already loved.

She wasn't the type to pick up a *People* magazine at the salon, and celebrities were too common around these parts to get excited or even notice one, especially when they didn't want to be noticed.

But that face demanded noticing.

They exchanged some lively banter, of course, because that was what Savannah Foster did best. He flirted, she volleyed, he hit on her, and she fell. Hard. And he happened to be staying in a swanky Santa Monica hotel right around the corner...

It wasn't until after she was naked and ready for round two that she realized "Nicky" was Nick Frye, television and movie star. Also...rather famously married to an Instagram model named Kalani Pele who was rumored to be some kind of Hawaiian royalty.

Furious and ashamed, she'd gathered up her clothes and dignity, but he snagged her on the way out, insisting his marriage was a sham. He and Kalani had been separated for six months, he claimed. The divorce papers were filed, he insisted. They wanted different things in life, he assured her.

We should have sex again, he whispered.

Oh, regrets and mistakes and bad, bad ideas... Savannah had her share of all of them, but Nick Frye? He was the king of all spontaneous bad decisions in her life. And apparently the king of the sperm, too, since on one of those two trips to paradise that Christmas night, Savannah conceived.

Either her IUD expired or that condom had a pinhole. Whatever happened, she was carrying Nick

Frye's son, and nearly lost the baby during that boating accident Ava had just described. It wasn't until that happened that Savannah decided to come clean with Nick, and face the fact that she fervently wanted this baby.

Except, she worried, so did he.

"You want to go in?" Mom asked as she put a gentle hand on Savannah's arm. A gentle, damp hand that was trembling ever so slightly. She must be pretty darn excited about finally getting a contractor for the B&B renovation.

Savannah eyed her mother, whose color seemed high, but then she was fair and it was blistering hot, and had been drinking a mimosa.

"I can get myself to the queen's bedroom," she assured her mother.

"I'll walk with you."

As much as Savannah wanted to gripe about the mothering being showered on her these days, she couldn't. With a partial placenta abruption caused by being in a boat that was slammed against storm-tossed waves, then flipped by a waterspout, Savannah needed all the help she could get to keep Junior locked in his room... or womb, as the case may be.

"Don't you want to show your new contractor around?" Savannah pushed herself up fairly easily, considering her seven-month belly.

Her mother glanced at Bill, currently in conversation with Kenny and Josh. "He's found some men to talk to."

"So the women can breathe a sigh of relief," Savannah joked. "Yeah, come on, walk me to the room and make sure Male Offspring doesn't fall out."

She laughed as she put an arm around Savannah. "He won't fall out, Sav."

"Hey, are you guys headed in?" Callie asked, coming over to Savannah's other side. "'Cause I'm going to catch a flight to Atlanta out of Key West."

Savannah turned to give her a hug. "Good to see you if only for a minute, counselor."

"Seriously, Savannah, I know you love a good nickname, but you really shouldn't call me that. I'm not a JD yet."

Savannah rolled her eyes. "Oh, darling little sister, do you never take a chill pill?"

Callie grinned, which only made her prettier. "I'll chill when I retire from the Supreme Court."

Mom gave a soft laugh and came around to give her youngest a hug. "If only you were kidding, child." With a kiss on Callie's nearly black hair, Mom inched back to look into her dark eyes with an adoring mother's gaze, making Savannah wonder if she would ever embrace motherhood with the same fervency.

"Thanks for your advice, honey," her mother said softly. "Using your freakishly high IQ for good things makes this mother happy."

"What advice did she give you?" Savannah asked, deeply curious.

"Just to...move on," Beck said. "Because it's time."

"Very smart," Savannah said. "It's nice to see you use your powers for good, not evil, future counselor. Are you sure you don't want to be a prosecutor?"

"And be poor and unknown my whole life?" Callie snorted. "I'm destined for big things in big law. Dad thinks I can clerk for a judge my first year of law school.

I'm actually taking a class in the fall because the visiting professor is married to a federal judge who I plan to impress the heck out of."

"Callie." Mom let out an exasperated sigh. "You have two more years of college. Enjoy them."

"Really, Cal," Savannah agreed. "Hit a frat party. Shotgun a beer. Be normal, for God's sake."

This time Callie rolled her eyes, just condescending enough for Savannah to know her baby sister would never make a dumb mistake like having sex with Nick Frye, super sperm shooter.

They said one more quick goodbye, and Savannah headed in with Mom.

"She's a piece of work," Savannah said. "In fact, she *is* work. Doesn't she ever get tired?"

"Mmmm."

"Whoa, I got a Beck Foster 'Mmmm.'" Savannah eyed her mother carefully. "What up, Mommy? You seem more than a one-mimosa-kind of distracted."

"I'm just...we have a new contractor," she said brightly.

"Yeah, that's great. Please don't let him start until I've found a place to live. I was counting on the contractor delay to allow me to stay until the baby is born."

Mom slid her a look as they walked into the downstairs bedroom suite that her mother had kindly given to Savannah so she could avoid three sets of stairs.

"Honey, if you think I'm going to kick you out before my grandson is born, you're crazy. Everyone will stay who wants to stay until we officially open Coquina House this Christmas. Kenny and Ava are moving soon to their rental house. There's plenty of room for you, Peyton, and me until we start taking guests. Then, you'll want to live with your son...somewhere."

Just the words pressed hard enough to make Savannah ease her baby-body onto the bed. Savannah had never stayed *anywhere* for more than a year once she'd moved away from her parents' Atlanta suburb home to attend Georgia State. She'd lasted there exactly three semesters, then decided to launch her life of adventure and world travel.

She'd spent her twenties moving, getting odd jobs, seeing new things and meeting new people. L.A. had just been the last stop, with dreams of New Zealand floating in her head.

But now? Well, she couldn't drag Thing One around like he was just another backpack. She couldn't even come up with a nickname for him and she was the reigning queen of nicknames.

"You look worried," Mom said, finally completely focused on Savannah. "You know I'm not going to let you spend one minute of uncertainty where this child is concerned."

"Too late," she said. "I live in a state of uncertainty. I'm the Mayor of Uncertainty. And you, dear mother, have a new B&B to build and run, a new contractor to order around, and a new life to seize as a single woman."

Mom patted her belly. "You're the one with a new life. You're literally growing one. Do you want me to get your phone so you can call Nick?"

She scowled. "Is it that obvious that's why I left the party?"

"You call him every day at the same time, returning

the call he made earlier in the day. I don't know who calls who at night, but I do hear you laughing in here."

"He makes me laugh." Dang she wished he didn't, but he did.

"That's a big change from when you first told us who fathered your child," Mom said. "There was no laughing that night."

"Ava was impressed." She chuckled, now able to laugh about the night a month ago when she broke the news to the same crew that was now outside on the veranda. "She wouldn't be if she knew it was not the great love affair I think she assumes it was. I couldn't fall quite that hard off the pedestal where that sixteen-year-old has permanently placed me. She doesn't need to know it was a one-night stand."

Mom sighed. "Sometimes good things come from one-night stands."

"Spoken like a true Mitchell-Ames-Foster woman, Mom." Savannah narrowed her eyes. "Do you ever think about yours?"

"My...what?"

"Your one-night stand. I mean, you brought Kenny into our lives and there's never been a whisper from either one of you who the father was."

Mom just stared at her and maybe paled a little, clearly uncomfortable with the subject.

"First of all, I didn't bring Kenny into our lives. Ava and her dearly departed grandmother deserve the credit. I gave him up for adoption and lived my life without spending too much time wondering about him."

"You don't want to talk about his father?"

"No, I don't, Savannah."

Which only made Savannah ache to know more. "Did Kenny want to know? Hasn't he asked you anything about him? I can't imagine not wondering."

"He hasn't...asked me." For some reason, it felt like Mom was choosing every word carefully.

"How did you keep Kenny's father away from the baby? I mean, I assume you told the guy." She pushed up a little, fascinated when she considered that her mother had faced the same problems Savannah had right now—a father who might not be welcome in a child's life. "Who *was* the guy?"

"No, Savannah, I'm not talking about it."

She lifted her brows, baffled by the reaction. Maybe she and Mom didn't tell each other *everything*, like Peyton and Mom seemed to do. But these past few months had been a big improvement for them. Their relationship, often contentious, sometimes confusing, had really smoothed over. But even with Kenny's arrival in their life, Mom had steadfastly avoided the topic of his father, claiming that the adoption was "sealed" and she owed him privacy.

"Okay, but can you tell me anything?" Savannah urged. "Was it a one-night stand?"

"I was fifteen when I got pregnant," she said, her voice taut. "Do fifteen-year-olds have one-night stands?"

"So he was your boyfriend?"

"I was dating him, much to Olivia's dismay," she added.

"Why?"

"He wasn't...her type."

"Let me guess, a bad boy?" Savannah grinned. "Oh, yes. Another Mitchell-Ames-Foster woman weakness."

Mom let out a quick laugh, not denying anything.

"Was he involved in the pregnancy? Agreed to the adoption?"

"Savannah." She breathed out the name with a weird kind of frustration. "He was a kid, probably scared out of his mind. Olivia made his parents, and him, sign things. It's...ancient history." Was it? Cause whoever this mystery boy from long ago was, it certainly made Mom tense to talk about him.

So, Savannah dialed it back and rolled onto her side. "This kid's gonna play soccer with all this kicking," she groaned, but secretly loved the sensation of feeling the baby's wee little limbs and grabby hands.

"Why don't you take a nap before you call Nick?" Mom suggested. "He'll get another break in shooting soon."

Savannah considered it, then shook her head. Truth was, she wanted to talk to Nick. She...liked talking to Nick. *Grrr.* "I keep thinking that this is the conversation when he'll tell me what he wants to do."

"What does he say he wants to do? Hasn't he given you any indication? Shared custody? Child support? Anything?"

"I've danced around the subject, and he side-steps. It's like..." Savannah shrugged, still not able to wrap her mind around what was going on with Nick. "It's like he's courting me, if I could be so old-fashioned."

"How so?"

"Our phone calls are like, well, like we're flirtatious and dating and talking about everything and nothing."

Mom looked as perplexed as Savannah felt. "He doesn't talk about the baby?"

"A little, to ask how I'm feeling or what the doctor said. I sent him an ultrasound picture and he decided the kid has his nose, which isn't a bad thing."

"But nothing about the future or his role in the baby's life?"

"No. But plenty about how his divorce will be final soon. Lot of that going around." She added with a playful wink. "I guess he's waiting until then to say anything. He hasn't told anyone, I don't think. And maybe that means he wants to keep the baby's identity or existence on the DL. Maybe his lawyers or agent or legions of publicists are putting together a plan. I don't know!" She let her frustration come out as she smacked the bed.

"Easy, honey," Mom said. "At least he's interested and friendly and not trying to pull some kind of weird stunt. He's taking it slow. And...courting you?"

"It just feels that way. I can't explain it. Like he's trying to get me to date him or something." She shrugged. "I honestly have no idea."

"What do you want him to do?" Mom asked, her voice serious enough that the question demanded some equally serious consideration.

"I think...I want him to be part of this kid's life. It seems fair to both of them. But I don't want to go back to L.A., I don't want to compromise my life or standards to fit his, and I don't want to be held hostage to his fame and fortune." She put her hand on her belly, a place that felt like home now. "But, more than anything, I want this child to be healthy, safe, secure, happy, and loved. And I kind of think his chances of that are better here in the company of this family, and not out in L.A. where the wild things are."

Mom nodded very slowly, listening. "I tend to agree. I don't know much about this Nick Frye guy, who seems... enigmatic in the press. I've googled him a bit and just can't get a handle on him."

"Well, I can tell you this. On our long daily conversations, he's nothing like I expected. Nothing. I kind of like him."

"That's encouraging."

"No it's not. It's terrifying."

Mom turned and looked at the dresser when Savannah's phone lit up and vibrated. With a smile, she stood and picked it up, glancing at the screen. "Well, Mr. Terrifying got tired of waiting for you to call."

Savannah sniffed a laugh. "I'm telling you, he's courting me."

Mom handed the phone to Savannah with a flourishing bow. "Your gentleman caller is on the line, m'lady."

Laughing, Savannah took it and touched the screen. Truth was, it was scary, but she didn't hate this. Not at all.

CHAPTER THREE
KENNY

"It's a gem, son." Bill gazed up at the back of Coquina House, studying the wide veranda, the row of windows around the other side, and the clapboard on the third floor. "The whole island is special. I guess I can see why you wanted to make it a permanent move. Kind of."

Kenny folded his arms and studied the man he thought he knew so well. But old Bill Dobson still had a few surprises in him, as this visit certainly proved.

"So, why'd you come down here, Bill?" he asked.

He hesitated for a second, then shrugged. "Hey, I took one look at the stuff you asked me to box up and ship before your move and it was easier to throw it all in the truck and drive here than pack that crap and take it to the post office."

Kenny slid him a glance. "Really."

"Really," he confirmed with a laugh. "You still have a whole house to move, son. This is enough to get you by until you do."

"I'm planning to go up soon and handle the details of that right before my house down here is ready for us to move in."

"So you're renting again?"

"Of course. I'll never get attached to another house after that fire. Ava and I got a great three-bedroom not too far from here, mid-island near a canal."

"That's good," Bill said, turning around to take in the whole property "So, you have the Atlantic on one side and then you cross the street to the canal front properties? Choice real estate, man. Must be worth a fortune."

"Lovely's owned it for years, along with quite a large parcel along the waterfront."

"So, when she wants to take out a big loan, it won't be a problem."

"Beck's going to try to pay cash," he said. "Unless she goes bigger than planned."

Bill grinned. "Bigger is always better, right?"

"Sometimes. You want to walk the inside of the house? I can show you the rough plans she's had drawn up."

Bill's eyes narrowed, a thin sheen of perspiration shining as they stood in the pounding heat. "How much money does she have?" he asked. "I mean, if she's going to pay cash."

Kenny flinched a little at the bluntness, which was usually couched in something a little more professional like "What's the budget and scope of the reno?" But this was Bill, and he didn't mince words.

"I know she wants the work to be high quality, but it's not a huge job. She wants to add a bedroom and bath in that third-floor space, and an en suite bath to one of the bedrooms on the second floor. That'll give her four guest suites, total, plus her own on the first floor. I could contract the work if I had a license in Florida. I have a temporary trade license, but she's going to need permits."

He nodded, considering that. "Still, not a huge GC job." He sounded disappointed that the profit wouldn't be massive, but, hey. He was the one who came down here uninvited and offered to take the job.

"Well, the kitchen's done," Kenny said. "And if you GC and I'm your foreman, I can slide into that permanent Florida contracting license. It would actually be great for me, workwise."

"Yeah," Bill said, a little distracted. "Did she pay you for the kitchen?"

Again, the question threw him. "I didn't take much because it was a favor for what she was doing for Ava, and we've been living here rent free."

"But she does own all this waterfront land, free and clear?" He let out a whistle. "Because, whoa, she's sitting on millions."

"Lovely owns it, I think. I haven't dug into her personal finances or how they've set up their partnership." He frowned at his friend. "Are you worried about getting paid, Bill? You don't have to. She paid the vendors net ten on every invoice, as far as I know."

His brows lifted as they walked toward the water to look out. "So, she must have done okay on that divorce she's celebrating."

"I don't know if she's celebrating, and I sure as hell don't know the details of the settlement, but I get the impression her ex was very generous." He snorted. "Should be, since there was another woman."

"Aw, the sweet young thing mid-life crisis fling, huh? And Beck wouldn't forgive him?"

"Actually, not a young thing, but his law partner. And if the rumor mill is correct, he's marrying the woman, so not exactly a mid-life crisis. But I don't know the details. This is just what Ava tells me. She hangs with the daughters a lot and picks up all kinds of gossip."

"Huh." He studied the house again, this time his gaze locked on the veranda where Beck was laughing with Jessie and Josh. He stared at her, his gaze seeming to drop over the tank top and shorts she wore and linger there a second or two too long. "Beautiful woman, that Beck Foster. Always was good-looking, but she's truly aged gracefully. Got a nice body and a pretty smile."

"*Annnd* we're talking about my birth mother. You do realize that?"

Bill gave one of his signature devil-may-care laughs and put a hand on Kenny's back. "I have not forgotten that, son. Now let's figure out how to make that pretty smile even brighter."

They climbed the stairs to join the others, who stopped talking when they reached the top.

"Beck, this house is as beautiful as you are," Bill said, walking toward her as if there were no other people on the big deck. "Please, take me around and show me everything you want to do." He put a casual hand on her bare shoulder and led her toward the sliders. "And tell me you're open to ideas because, honey, I've got so many of them."

She gave a slightly self-conscious laugh and glanced over her shoulder at Josh, who leaned against the railing holding a beer, his half smile firmly in place. Of course, he'd be happy today. He'd been waiting for that divorce to be signed and everyone there knew that, even if they didn't have Ava to provide the inside scoop like Kenny did.

Everyone but Bill, who still had a familiar hand on Beck's back as they headed inside. Bill wasn't a player or a flirt, Kenny thought. He'd barely dated anyone since his own divorce, which had been a hot, hot mess since Natalie had some serious problems. But he sure looked like a man on the move right now, and that was enough to make Kenny decide to accompany them on this tour.

Not that Beck needed protection or supervision, but Kenny would be the on-site tradesman who'd manage the subs in Bill's absence. Unless Bill stayed to manage the job himself.

He never did say why he'd come here, did he?

"I think I'll join them, too," Lovely said, coming up next to Kenny with a smile. "He seems to have forgotten there are two clients on this job."

Kenny and Lovely headed into the kitchen, where Bill was admiring the work—the same work Kenny had shown him when he first got here.

"Love that farmhouse sink," Bill said, running his hand along the white porcelain. "And what a view." But he seemed to be more fascinated by Beck than the water.

"We have it from almost every one of the guest rooms, or will, when we finish the third floor," Beck said, coolly stepping away to slide an arm around her mother. "This woman has lived in or near this house for seventy-three years, Bill, so if you want to capture the history, Lovely knows it all."

"There's no way you're seventy-three," he said with a

twinkle in his eye. "With purple streaks in your hair." He inched closer. "They suit you."

She gave a musical laugh at the compliment. "Courtesy of our darling Ava."

"Isn't she the greatest kid?" he asked both ladies, giving Kenny an odd sense of relief that at least Bill was spreading his charm beyond just Beck. She didn't need to be swept off her feet by a man she hadn't seen in forty years, not that Beck seemed like the type to be "swept" anyway.

But as Kenny followed the trio through the house, he couldn't help but see Bill in a different light than he did when they were on a job site. He seemed to have a sort of magical attraction that had both women looking up at him, cracking up at his jokes, and enthusiastically describing their renovation plans. And he was like the dream contractor, asking all the right questions, coming up with new ways of looking at the building process, and closing the deal with grace and ease.

Could he really just have left his business and at least two or three houses that couldn't be quite finished yet, just to bring Kenny his stuff and do the favor of filing permits and being the "acting" contractor?

Yes, Bill was a good guy. This would help Beck and, really, it would help Kenny secure his own license. But truly, this visit went above and beyond good. That was great. And for some reason, Kenny just didn't quite buy it.

"Remember how we did that wet room in the Huntington house, Ken?" Bill asked, dragging him back into the conversation. "You think we could do a scaled-down version up here?"

"What's a wet room?" Beck asked. "Because it sounds like something we have after a hurricane."

Bill cracked up. "Good one." Then his face grew serious. "You get those bad down here, don't you?"

"They have been known to hit," she said. "And we're in the heart of the season, now, so you should take storm delays into consideration for the schedule."

"What do you do for a storm like that?" Bill asked. "Do you have hurricane shutters?"

"We have window and door boards in storage," Lovely told him. "And a safe room on the first floor. And we're hardy. Storms happen down here, and we survive."

"I see that," he said, admiring the oversized attic, currently decorated as one massive bedroom with a small, unattractive bathroom. "You want to add a bedroom and bath in this area?" he asked.

"That's what we hoped, and we had some rudimentary plans drawn up. Enough that you could probably start pulling together an estimate."

Still thinking, he walked to the wall, peering out a small window.

"We could add a window for the second bedroom," Beck said, as if she sensed he didn't love her plan.

"You could knock this wall out, put sliders in and add another balcony, make a massive bedroom with a sitting area, and that spa bathroom with the wet room. Your guests would have an unobstructed ocean view, a private veranda, and you could charge a fortune."

Oh, yes, Bill thought...big, Kenny mused. Always a little outsized of what a client thought he or she wanted.

Beck's brows lifted. "But it would give me one less

bedroom. I really think I need four to make this a viable B&B."

"And what would that cost?" Lovely asked. "It sounds frightfully expensive."

"It's not cheap," Bill conceded. "And you can run the numbers on what kind of income a luxury suite would bring over two small rooms. But I really think you could turn this phenom space into a massive honeymoon suite or a presidential palace, so much more than a couple of rooms in the Keys." He grinned. "Now that, ladies, is what we call an *event*."

Beck and Lovely looked at each other, silent communication bouncing between them, no doubt both enthralled with the idea...and the idea-giver.

"We'll have to think about it," Beck said. "When do you need to know?"

"As soon as possible, if you want me on the job," Bill replied, a slow smile growing. "We need plans, permits, trades, and a timeline."

Beck's eyes grew wide, her excitement palpable. "We could make this attic really amazing, Lovely."

"I know," the other woman agreed. "Let's go sit down with our calculator and make some decisions."

They both started walking out, chatting quietly as they tossed Bill's ideas back and forth.

"You really think that's the way to go in this space?" Kenny asked.

"Without a doubt."

Kenny had doubts, many of them. "But will that over-the-top suite fit the Coconut Key vibe? I'm not sure. People don't come to the Keys for luxury. They want a view, good fishing, and a lot of margaritas, not grand ideas."

Bill cocked his head. "I'm thinking about profits, son. Grand ideas bring grand profits."

Beck called a question to Bill and he headed out to answer it, moving with that calm, cool confidence he exuded.

Grand profits, huh? For Beck...or him?

Kenny really didn't want his loyalties put to the test between these two people...who were both, he had to remember, more than his friends. They were his parents.

CHAPTER FOUR
PEYTON

*J*essie didn't look the least bit surprised when she came into her office in the back of Chuck's, the high-end restaurant she owned, and found Peyton occupying her seat.

"Crazy times at Coquina House?" Jessie guessed.

"Between the designer, trades, the bed rest pregnant sister, the bored teenager ready to start school, and stressed-out Mom and Lovely now that they actually have a contractor and the reno is real? Things have really escalated this past week." Peyton laughed but the truth was, she knew it was time to find a place to live and work, but something was holding her back.

But wasn't that the story of Peyton Foster's life? Waiting for something...only to have it slip away? The perfect man, the perfect job...and now, the perfect place to live in the Keys.

"Well, you're always welcome here, but the restaurant is open tonight." Jessie dropped into the other seat. "Never fear, we only have a rocking four reservations."

"It's the wrong season, Jess," Peyton said quickly, knowing that a low-grade worry about money and restaurant profits was always gnawing away at Jessica Donovan. "I've never seen Coconut Key so empty. Or felt anything quite this hot and humid. Even the beach is unbearable."

"I know, I know," Jessie agreed, curling a tendril of her dark hair around a finger. "It's August in Florida, there are a couple of storms brewing off the coast of Africa, and my regular locals all seem to be more interested in the competition."

"Oh. *Him*." Peyton tried to make light of it, but Tag Jadrien, the renowned chef in Key West, had opened up Coconut Tropics, a satellite restaurant right here on the island, and had taken a big bite out of Jessie's business.

Last month, Tag had made an offer to buy Chuck's, and Peyton was afraid Jessie was tempted to take it, especially since he'd increased the money.

"Are you ready to give up your dream, Jessie?" Peyton asked. "The restaurant you named for your dearly departed husband?"

"The restaurant I was only able to open because he left me insurance money?" She gave a wistful smile. "He'd be furious. Especially since it is Tag who made the offer to buy it."

"That's right, the love triangle from your youth. Tag was the loser."

Jessie looked away, her eyes cloudy as they usually were when the conversation turned to the husband she'd lost about four years ago. But she seemed even more uncomfortable than usual—something Peyton had noticed when the topic included Tag Jadrien.

Peyton wished the other woman would confide more.

Jessie, who'd been Mom's childhood best friend until they were ten and separated by time and distance, had become more than Peyton's boss and mentor; she was truly a friend.

But Peyton definitely sensed Jessie was holding back on this subject. Did Lovely know the whole story of Tag and Chuck? Lovely had been close to Jessie all these years —a neighbor who became a dear friend. So, Peyton made a mental note to ask her, although Lovely had proven she was an ace secret keeper.

"How goes the cookbook war?" Jessie asked, shifting her attention to the galleys spread over her desk.

"Getting close to going off to a formatter, which is our next major step in production."

Nodding, Jessie studied the printed pages and the old-school hand markings Peyton had made.

"Formatting's done by computer," Peyton told her. "But I did learn to check galleys the old way when I worked for a textbook publisher. I promise you these changes will..." She looked up and noticed a faraway look on Jessie's face. "Will never be made and the book will be riddled with typos."

Jessie nodded, making Peyton poke her. "Hello, earth to Chef Donovan?"

She managed a smile. "Sorry. Drifting. Pey, maybe I should take the money and...relieve all of us." Jessie barely whispered the last word, spoken so softly that Peyton wasn't even sure she'd heard her.

"I wouldn't be relieved," Peyton said, reaching out to her. "You can't turn this place over to Tag Jadrien without giving it the old college try. I will be right there with you, making it happen."

"You're the best, Peyton." She angled her head and looked hard at Peyton. "And how are you doing these days? I get so involved, I forget you're nursing a heartbreak. No word from Val, huh?"

She leaned back and looked at the door like he would walk back in any minute, a faint smell of shrimp clinging to his clothes and a few bad fish jokes at the ready.

But Valentino Sanchez wasn't coming back. The gorgeous fisherman who'd stolen her heart hadn't even called her once since the day he said goodbye right out in Chuck's parking lot. He'd shocked her with news that he was an accountant, not a fisherman, and needed to go back to Miami to finally deal with the pain of losing his fiancée.

"No, and for once in my life, I'm not waiting. I'm doing something." She gestured toward the cookbook, wishing it were true. But the fact was, Peyton still checked her phone for that call.

"He'll be back," Jessie said, but her voice lacked any hint of enthusiasm.

"You don't believe that and neither do I," Peyton said. "I think he'd have called or texted or sent a smoke signal by now. It's been..." She made a face, ashamed to report she still counted days. Thirty-four of them to be precise. "Over a month."

"He loved it here and was building a great business. I can't believe he'd just..." She pulled her phone out of her pocket when it rang with a call. "Oh, it's my little sister, Heather."

"The one who taught you to make scones? Tell her I said thank you," Peyton said.

"I will." She gave the phone another look. "I hope everything's okay up there."

She pushed off the chair and walked toward the door, her last ominous words making Peyton recall that Heather, Jessie's younger half-sister who lived in Charleston, was married to a man who'd been battling cancer. Peyton said a silent prayer and went back to the galleys, listening for laughter or chatter from Jessie in the kitchen, but she didn't hear a thing.

When Jessie came back in, her face was wet with tears, her eyes red, and immediately Peyton came around the desk to reach for her. Jessie dropped her head on Peyton's shoulder and let a sob out.

"He passed overnight. They'd found another brain tumor, but it was inoperable."

"Oh, God." Suddenly all her problems and waiting and frustrations seemed so small and inconsequential. "How's Heather doing?"

"She's a wreck. Thirty-eight years old, two teenagers, a café to run, and oh..." She swallowed a sob. "I have to go up there and help her."

"Of course you do. You're her sister."

"I wish we'd been closer all these years," Jessie said, pulling back to wipe her eyes while Peyton reached for a tissue. "I mean, there's no bad blood, but she's so much younger than I am, and we had a different mother..." She groaned. "When my dad left, he never came back here. I made a few trips up to see him but I was around eighteen when they had Heather. She always seemed more like a niece than a sister. Drew, her husband? Such a solid guy. He did everything to help her make that little café a success. I can't believe he's gone."

Grief and shock had her babbling now, blowing her nose, processing the loss.

Peyton reached out and hugged her again. "I can hold down the fort while you help her. As long as you need. I know your vendors, your orders, and how to do most anything around here when the restaurant is closed."

"I should close?"

"Why not? Take a summer break like lots of businesses do in the Keys. I'll work from here, answer your phones, take care of business. You won't have to even think about it."

Jessie's eyes cleared for a moment. "Would you really do that for me?"

"Of course, Jessie. Did you call Josh?" Her brother would be just as distraught, no doubt.

She shook her head. "I don't want to tell him over the phone. He liked Drew. I want to go over to his shop and tell him in person."

"Go do that then," Peyton said. "Do you want me to go with you?"

She thought about it for a second. "Could you call the four reservations we have and cancel? And contact the staff? And any vendors or meetings? I need to check out."

"I got this, girl." Peyton added a kiss on Jessie's hair, but the look she got in response was dark with worry.

"You know I'll be dead broke if this place has no revenue for a few weeks," she said in a raspy voice.

"Jessie," Peyton said. "Life's too short to worry."

Jessie put a hand on Peyton's cheek, searching her face, silent for a moment. "It's too short to wait, too."

With one more hug, Jessie left, leaving Peyton fighting her own tears.

CHAPTER FIVE
BECK

*A*s Beck sat on her usual perch in the woodworking studio, watching Josh carve a fireplace mantle, she suddenly realized how much she'd missed spending time with him. All her focus had been on planning the renovation now that they had a contractor.

She listened to him tell her about the house where the piece would be going, his voice the same mix of gentle and strong as his hands.

"I had no idea you got that business, Josh. I remember when you met with the owner and did some drawings."

He gave her a wry smile. "You've been awfully busy with the reno and Bill and all."

"I know I have, and I'm sorry about that."

"Why?" He looked up. "You've waited a long time for the right contractor and here he is."

His blue eyes had a little spark as he asked the question, a little amusement but maybe it was something else.

Maybe it was a teeny bit of jealousy. Which wouldn't be completely unwarranted.

Josh and Beck seemed to balance on the precipice of...something. Yes, they'd kissed once. Yes, she "bought" a date at a bachelor auction but hadn't yet cashed in on that donation. And yes, she'd promised him that when the divorce was final, they'd take the next natural step in their budding relationship.

"So how's it going at Coquina House?" he asked. "You're still certain you want to do the Grand Salon upstairs?"

"The Grand...who calls it that?"

"Kenny," he said without hesitation. "He said it's typical Bill Dobson overkill, the way he does everything."

"Overkill? Kenny has worked for Bill for a long time. He thinks Bill's renos are fantastic. He's told me that many times, and have you seen the pictures on his website? He does the whole farmhouse chic like no one else."

He held his spokeshave tool up to stop her. "Methinks you doth protest too much."

She laughed. "I love it when you quote Shakespeare."

"Son of a bookstore owner," he joked. "But, seriously, Beck. It's your house, do what you want. And Kenny does respect Bill's work, I just think he and Maggie aren't sure it's the right way to go."

"Let me get this straight," she said. "My son and my designer are second-guessing my decisions and talking to you about that?"

"Chill, mama. Kenny's my friend and Maggie's his..."

"More than friend," she supplied with a smile.

"And we all want you to make smart decisions, but they are *your* decisions."

She settled back on the chair, her concerns quieted for the moment. Mostly because that's what Josh did—he calmed her with his clear thinking and steadiness. "They do really seem to like each other," she mused, her mind going back to Kenny and Maggie. "He's been with her a lot lately."

"Does that bother you?" he asked, crouching down to brush some sawdust off the top of the mantle and examine his work.

"Of course not."

"Does it bother Ava?"

She considered that, thinking of comments Ava had made on the topic. "I don't know," she said. "Ava is so focused on starting school this fall and that new driver's license she has."

"You don't think she's jealous of her father's new girl-friend?" he pressed.

"Girlfriend? They aren't *that* serious, are they?"

"Just dating, as far as I can tell, but that's a big move for Kenny," he added.

"I didn't realize you were that close to him, Josh."

"We spend a decent amount of time together," he said. "Less since Bill came, because those two seem to have a lot in common."

Like the fact that they were father and son. She shifted on her chair, a little uncomfortable with not telling Josh the truth. But was it her truth to tell? With a man she was thinking about dating? Maybe it was.

"Kenny told me he hasn't been involved with anyone since his wife died five years ago," Josh said. "So, that's why I'm wondering about Ava. Her dad seeing someone is new for her."

"Gosh, I haven't really talked to her about it," Beck said, kicking herself for letting yet another important person get ignored while she got wrapped up in the reno. "How sweet of you to think of her that way." But why would that surprise Beck? Josh was a thoughtful man, quietly worrying about everyone but himself. "I'll have to make a mental note to have that conversation with Ava."

"Well, you've been *very* busy lately," he said, with just a hint of a tease, but also a little hurt. And the last person on earth she wanted to hurt was Josh.

"Like I said, I'm sorry for going MIA."

"I don't mind...much." He slid into that slow smile she liked so much. "Unless I'm losing you to something more threatening than the renovation."

"Threatening?" Her heart slid around a bit, making her stand and take a few steps closer to him. Should she tell him the truth? Should she saddle him with a secret—especially one that might make him even more uncertain about her relationship with Bill?

He stood, too, eclipsing her five-feet-five with his full six, looking down with those kind blue eyes she'd come to want to see every day since she moved to Coconut Key.

"He likes you," he said simply.

Oh, boy. "I'm his client, Josh. And he's...flirtatious. A big personality. The kind of guy that likes to be the center of attention."

"Your attention."

She had to tell him, but she'd have to clear it with Kenny first. And as soon as she did, she was telling Josh the whole truth. Under the right circumstances, at the right time, with her son's permission.

"Speaking of attention..." She placed a playful finger on his chest. "Did you forget I bought one at that bachelor auction?"

"Forget? You're kidding, right?"

That made her smile. "So, how about this weekend?"

He studied her for a long time, not moving, not looking away. "Yes."

The answer, simple, straightforward, and so...Josh, just made her smile. She looked up at him, drawn to his sky-blue eyes and—

"Josh?" Jessie's voice floated in from the front showroom, followed by footsteps, loud and fast enough for them both to separate.

"Back here, Jess," he called.

The minute Beck saw Jessie, she knew something was very wrong. She went right to her friend, who'd been crying, but Jessie's red-rimmed eyes stayed on Josh.

"Bad news, brother," she whispered. "Drew didn't make it."

His whole face crumbled, along with his shoulders, bending over as if he'd been hit. "Oh, man. No."

Instantly, Jessie and Josh went to each other, hugging as the loss hit, while Beck remembered all Jessie had told her about her brother-in-law, who was younger than Kenny. She knew he'd had a brain tumor removed, but they'd found another, so this was the worst possible outcome.

After a moment, they turned to her and she reached out to hold them and murmur words of sympathy.

"We have to go up," Jessie said, wiping her eyes. "Not

just for the funeral, which is in a few days, but to help Heather get on her feet."

"Absolutely," Josh replied without a moment's hesitation. "Let's drive. We can leave tomorrow morning and be there by six to do whatever she needs."

Beck found herself smiling at the solidarity of the family, even one made distant by different mothers, many years, and a few hundred miles. She hoped her girls would be as rock solid and generous with their time.

"I'll call Heather," Jessie said, pulling out her phone. "Do you want to talk to her?"

"Of course." Josh turned to Beck as Jessie dialed, giving her a different sad look. "Rain check?" he asked, reaching for her hand.

"Without a doubt." And she'd tell him the truth about Bill the minute they could talk privately. Until then, she was keeping a secret from him, and she knew firsthand that was a recipe for disaster.

WHEN BECK GOT BACK to Coquina House, she was surprised to find it feeling empty and quiet, since she thought Bill and Kenny's meeting with the electrician would still be underway. But when she heard laughter from Savannah's room, she headed there, finding her daughter playing gin rummy with Ava.

She filled them in on the sad news, telling them what she knew about Drew Monroe, talking in hushed tones about life and death, but not too much because the subject made Ava blue.

"How old are the kids?" Ava asked.

"I know they're teenagers," Beck said. "I think Madison is your age, and Marc is a little younger."

She made a face. "Poor kids."

"Well, you're being a good babysitter, Ava," Beck said, nodding toward the card game.

"She better be," Savannah said. "She's number one backup for Boyo."

"Don't you have a better nickname for him yet?" Beck asked. "You have a nickname for the mailman, for heaven's sake."

"You mean Jay Leno?" At Beck's look, she added, "What? Have you seen his chin?"

Beck had to laugh despite the mood, as Ava and Savannah picked up the cards to resume the game. "Where's your dad, Ava? I thought he and Bill were going to have a meeting with the electrician today."

"They did already," she said. "I think Bill was going to meet with some friends of his in Key West and Dad's buying paint."

"Paint?" Beck frowned. "I haven't picked any colors yet."

"It's not for this house. He wants to paint the bathrooms in our new rental. The owner said it was okay, and that's what he wants to do." She sounded a little miffed at the idea. "I liked mine pink, but Maggie said it looked like the 'underbelly of a pig.'" She mocked the term with a very unhappy face.

Ahhh. Maggie. Of course Josh, a sensitive and intuitive man, was right about that issue.

Savannah snorted. "Pig Underbelly. I like it."

"Well, Maggie didn't."

"She's a designer," Beck reminded her gently. "And her taste is impeccable."

Ava rolled her eyes. "Pigs are cute," she said, suddenly sounding more like six than sixteen. "Anyway, that's where he is. Painting bathrooms with Maggie." She picked up a card, stuck it in her hand, then dropped another face down on the pile. "And that is ginerooski, as you would say, Savannah."

"What?" Savannah pushed up, blinking. "You needed that six of hearts? How did I not know that?"

As they negotiated the fine points of their rummy match, Beck tried to decide how best to approach the issue of how Ava felt about her father dating again. How she felt about Maggie in particular, and this new change in her ever-changing life in general.

Maybe Kenny had been absolutely right in not telling Ava about Bill. The poor kid did have a lot going on.

"What color did Maggie recommend?" Beck asked when Savannah accepted defeat and Ava started shuffling.

"Something blue or turquoise or...I don't know. She said it was 'reminiscent of the sea' so, whatever."

Ava studied her granddaughter, happy to see that diamond in her nose was a thing of the past, replaced by a smattering of freckles she'd earned from the summer sun. Just sixteen a few days ago, she'd lost a bit of the edge she'd arrived with, softening in her tone and dress and even how she carried herself. She seemed happier, and that was all Beck wanted.

Would Maggie Karras dating Ava's father change that?

"Am I crazy to say I hear a teeny bit of resentment in

your voice?" Beck asked softly. "Like maybe you wanted a different color on your bathroom walls?"

"Or a different..." She didn't finish the sentence, studying the deck of cards she shuffled.

"Ava?" Beck coaxed. "Something bothering you?"

"Nope." She slapped the cards together and looked up. "One more hand, Savannah Banana?"

Savannah slowly shook her head. "I want to know why you're all tense now."

She whistled out a noisy breath. "I'm just...you know."

"If we knew, we wouldn't ask," Savannah said, putting her hand over the deck of cards, obviously one hundred percent in tune with what Beck was thinking. "Tell us what's bothering you, grasshopper."

She looked up at Savannah, her expression softening. "I don't want to be a cliché," she said.

"They are the worst," Savannah agreed.

"Why would you be a cliché?" Beck asked.

"Being the bratty teenager who can't stand her dad's new girlfriend. I don't want to be that...predictable."

Savannah and Beck shared a quick, silent glance.

"Are you having issues with your dad seeing Maggie?" Beck put a hand on Ava's arm. "Because sometimes clichés are clichés for a reason—they're very real and natural feelings."

Ava didn't answer for a moment, fluttering the cards in her hand. "I just..." She groaned softly. "Look, it doesn't take a shrink. She's not my mom. My dad's kind of ga-ga over her with 'Maggie says this' and 'Maggie does that' and 'Maggie knows all' and...you get the idea."

"Maggie the Magnificent," Savannah joked.

"And she's fine, really. Nice lady. Very kind. She's...*fine*.

As far as women Dad could date go, she's...fine." She gave a soft laugh at how many times she'd said that, then her expression grew serious. "I'm just scared."

"Of losing him?" Beck guessed.

"Of him forgetting Mom," she answered with a hitch in her voice. "I'm scared that Elise Gallagher will just be... gone." She blinked, fighting tears. "And I don't want her to ever be gone."

"Of course not." Beck reached in for another hug, giving it whether Ava wanted one or not. She'd arrived as a self-proclaimed "not a hugger." But she hugged now and didn't seem to hate it. "You never want to forget her."

"So what do I do?" Ava asked. "I really don't want to be a baby about it. Dad's been amazing. He quit his jobs and moved us here and I know all that was for me. Yeah, he likes Maggie, but I don't think he did that for her." She frowned. "Did he?"

"Of course not," Beck assured her. "He made that decision because he saw the positive, healthy changes in you and knew that we're the family you need. Maggie was just a..."

"Side benefit," Savannah suggested.

But Ava shook her head. "He really likes her, though. He's never liked anyone. If he's had a date since Mom died, I didn't know about it." She put the cards down. "I swear on the Bible—and that's not something my mother or Grandma Janet would let me do if I didn't mean it—I don't want my dad *not* to have a girlfriend. But I just don't want my mom to disappear into thin air."

The ache in her voice tore Beck's heart. "She never will, Ava. You can keep her alive."

"How? The more Maggie's around, the less...he remembers her."

"I bet that's not true," Savannah said gently. "I bet he's remembering your mother more than ever, and maybe even feeling a little guilty about having feelings for someone else. Your parents were like high school sweethearts, right?"

"Mom used to tell me that neither of them ever kissed anyone else," she said, then snorted softly. "Guess that's not true anymore."

Beck took a slow breath and dug into her box of motherhood tools, trying to think of the best way to help Ava navigate this.

"You know what I think?" she asked. "I believe Maggie is a little tense about it all, too."

"Has she told you that?" Ava asked.

"Not in so many words, but what I know of Maggie tells me she wouldn't want your mother's memory to disappear, either. She probably wants to honor it and acknowledge what an amazing person your mother was, and that will help her understand and love you and your dad."

The frown lessened a little. "You really think so?"

"I do," Beck assured her. "And I think the way to help that happen is for you to be the one who shares things about your mom. You keep that memory alive, and I bet that Maggie will help you. Your dad might be uncomfortable because men don't really..."

"Have brains," Savannah finished, making them both laugh.

"They aren't quite as in touch with their emotions," Beck continued. "Kenny's probably terrified that talking about your mom would send Maggie running, but it's just the opposite. Knowing what he and you loved about her will help Maggie understand you better."

"Deep, Mom," Savannah teased, but Ava shook her head.

"I know what you mean, Grandma Beck," Ava said. "She asked me something the other day about my mom and I didn't really answer because I thought she was just making small talk."

"Well, next time you should make that small talk big," Savannah suggested. "When will there be a next time?"

She crinkled her nose. "They invited me to help them paint today but I thought they were just being nice."

"Did your dad invite you, or Maggie?" Beck asked.

"Actually, it was Maggie."

Beck angled her head and conjured up her best "I told you so" face. "Why don't you go over there right now and help them?"

"You think I should?"

"You can take my car," Savannah said. "You're the one who got her license last week."

"Really?" She looked from one to the other, brighter. "Okay. I will. Thanks." She set the cards on top of Savannah's baby bump. "Will you be okay playing solitaire?"

Savannah laughed. "I'll survive. Go. The keys are in my purse."

"Actually, I think they're still in mine," Ava said on a laugh. "Bye, you guys!"

She was gone in a flash, and Beck sighed, watching the empty doorway. "We forget about all the things that churn inside you at sixteen."

But Savannah was shaking her head.

"No? What?" Beck was confused by her daughter's bewildered expression.

"I just have so much to learn about being a mom," she said. "How'd you do that?"

"Years of experience raising daughters."

But Savannah just sighed. "I just hope I'm half the mom you are, Rebecca Foster."

Beck smiled, her heart folding in half at the compliment. "Well, you better get to work on a nickname for that boy, then."

CHAPTER SIX
KENNY

*H*e wanted to tell her. He wanted to tell her everything.

That's when Kenny Gallagher knew he was in trouble with Maggie Karras. He wanted to tell her the truth about Bill being his biological father, and the way he felt about losing his wife. He wanted to share how he woke up in the middle of the night in a cold sweat worried about his teenage daughter, and, oh, man, he wanted her to know how much it hurt to have had, and lost, a son. He wanted to *talk*, which was crazy since Ken Gallagher had kept his mouth shut and his feelings buried for five solid years.

In fact, words were threatening to come bubbling out as big and bold as the dark green paint Maggie convinced him to use on the master bathroom walls.

Was this burning need to communicate normal? After about half a dozen dates and countless hours working together, shouldn't his thoughts be a little lower than the brain and mouth? Yeah, he wanted to sleep with Maggie.

Every time they kissed and she pressed her body against his, he wanted that. They hadn't yet, but it would surely happen when he had his own place and wasn't living at Coquina House.

But more than sex, he wanted to talk.

The very idea was flat out terrifying.

"You're not painting." Maggie turned from the window, the light like a halo around her dark hair, her eyes, also nearly black, dancing with mirth. "You're watching me paint. That's not fair."

"You're so good at it. And fun to watch."

She leaned over to dip the brush in the paint can. "Trimming is an art," she said lightly. "But that roller is way more satisfying. Wanna switch?"

He didn't move, still leaning against the unpainted wall behind him, arms crossed, thinking...about talking.

"What?" she asked, looking up, a smile pulling on her very pretty features. "What's going on in that head of yours, Kenneth Gallagher?"

Maybe he should start with something simple. Not secrets, no sadness, no things that kept him awake.

"What do you think of Bill?" he asked.

Her brows flicked up at the question, but she didn't answer right away. Instead, she dabbed the brush in the paint, slid it along the side of the can, then returned to edge the window frame. "I think he's hiding something."

Damn right he was—the fact that they were related. "Really. How so?"

"I don't know, he's sort of a jester type, you know? Hides behind jokes and flirting."

"He flirts with *you*?"

She threw him a look over her shoulder. "Easy, boy. And no, he's been nothing but professional. He flirts with Beck. A lot."

Because he remembers...the Camaro.

Uncomfortable with that thought, he finally pushed off the wall to snag the roller and start painting. "I guess he thinks she's attractive," he said.

"She is. Warm and kind and excited about this B&B. I like Beck," she said simply. "And not just because she's your birth mother. Is that weird, by the way, or have you two come to terms with that whole...history?"

They had come to terms but then Bill showed up. "It's fine," he said. Funny, he didn't want to talk about *that*. "She's great with Ava."

Maggie made a sound that was more like a soft grunt or moan.

"She's not good with Ava?"

"She's great with her, yeah. In fact..." Maggie sighed. "They have a great connection. Savannah, too. Those two are more like sisters than aunt and niece."

He finally rolled the paint, watching it cling to the beige behind it. "My mother knew what she was doing, sending Ava to find Beck. Not sure I appreciate having my kid find her way to the Keys, but somehow my mother knew if Ava found my birth mother, she'd have a chance. She knew that kid needed a strong woman in her life."

Maggie didn't respond, just turned and got more paint on her brush.

"So, for that, I'm grateful," he finished. "No matter how weird the situation was." Or currently was, thanks to Bill.

"Was Elise strong?" she asked softly, her voice like a tap on the door to his heart, trying to get in. Okay, then. *Here's your chance, boyo.*

"Yeah, she was one of those people that could handle anything and everything, like life was...effortless." He smiled, thinking about it. "She had a to-do list for every day, at least four active calendars and those desk planner things, and all manner of organizational tools."

"So she was structured, but that's not the same as strong."

He frowned, considering that. "But she was strong. Nothing fazed her. Not motherhood, not financial stuff, not messed-up people."

"I wonder how she got that way," Maggie mused, a hint of envy in her voice. "Some days I wake up and wonder what will faze me next."

"Her faith," he said, without a second's hesitation.

Maggie slowed her brush and looked at him. "Really?"

"Yes, really. She walked..." *With the Lord.* He caught himself before saying that out loud because he knew she'd probably laugh at him. Nobody talked like that unless they were in church, a place he hadn't been in a long, long time. "Straight," he finally finished.

"So, she was religious?"

He almost laughed just thinking about how much Elise hated that word. "She was a Christian," he corrected, more out of honor for his late wife than having to make a point to Maggie. That was how she always answered when someone called her *religious*.

"Oh, I didn't know."

"No reason you would." He bent over to slather the roller in more paint.

"Are you?" she asked. "Religious, I mean."

Now there was the fifty-thousand-dollar question. "Not...anymore."

"But you were?" she pressed.

"We met through our church as teenagers," he said as if that said it all.

"But you outgrew it, I assume."

Outgrew? Not exactly how he'd describe his falling out of faith. "I don't pray, if that's what you mean." Unless railing at God for being so unfair could be considered praying. 'Cause he still did that on some particularly dark nights.

"I grew up in a Greek orthodox home," she said, painting again.

"How was that?"

"In some ways, comforting. The rituals, you know. We Greeks love our rituals. And food. And, oh so many hours at St. Katherine's. But mostly, I found religion suffocating and stifling. Of course, I left it all behind the minute I could think for myself."

A feeling he didn't quite understand bubbled up inside him—like the need to defend that very God who he'd tried to ignore for the past five years. "It can be stifling," he said. "Or it can be...nice."

"Nice if you're a sheep." She held up her hand in apology. "Sorry. Didn't mean it that way. I know you were married to someone religious, so —"

"She *wasn't* religious," he said, unable to tamp down the frustration. "That means something else completely."

Drawing back, she made a face. "Are we having our first fight?"

"No, Maggie, we're not fighting."

She eyed him for a minute, a smile pulling. "You still have a long way to go, you know."

What the hell did that mean?

"To get over her," she added, as if she had heard what he was thinking.

"I don't want to get over her," he said. "I just want to remember her and...find...something."

On a sigh, she bent over and carefully set the paintbrush on the tarp next to the can. "What?"

"I said I—"

She straightened and put her hand over his lips, stopping him. "What is that something you're looking for? I need to know."

He searched her face for a long moment, a little lost in the depth of those dark eyes, but they didn't look inviting right now. They looked...challenging.

"I'm looking for someone to talk to," he whispered, his voice ragged with honesty. "About life and Ava and work and the world and, yeah, God. Whatever. Someone who could be a partner and friend and lover and...whatever. Girlfriend." He angled his head. "Is that you, Maggie?"

"Out of that list, I'll take lover and see what develops from there."

Not friend? Not partner? Not girlfriend? Yes, he had an awful lot of baggage and history that was probably too much for her. So why not take what she was offering?

"I could start there," he said slowly, knowing that deep inside him, that wasn't *all* he wanted.

Just as she got up on her tiptoes to kiss him, a noisy knock at the front door stopped her.

"Hold that thought," he said. "And this roller."

Giving it to her, he headed down the hall and through the living room, smiling when he saw Ava cupping her hands on the sidelight to the front door peering in. How would Maggie feel about this, he wondered? Were kids as stifling and suffocating as God to this woman who chose "lover" out of his list of options?

"Hey, A." He opened the door, warmed by that smile that just seemed to grow brighter since they'd made the decision to move down here. "Change your mind about painting?"

"Yep. Is that okay?"

"It's awesome." Maybe not the best timing...but then, maybe it was.

She stepped inside and dangled the car keys. "Plus, Savannah let me drive her car. I like having a license, Dad."

He smiled, still amazed this was the same girl paralyzed by left turns when she was learning. "Come on in. We're doing my bathroom first."

Ava followed him down the hall, coming to a freezing stop when they reached the bathroom. "Whoa. Green."

"It's actually called cilantro." Maggie turned and smiled. "Which a lot of people hate."

"The food, yes?" Ava said, stepping in and checking out the half-rolled wall. "The color isn't so bad. It's kind of...manly."

"That's good," Maggie said. "We were going for dramatic but masculine. And I absolutely love turquoise for your bathroom, Ava. I picked Rapture Blue."

Ava chuckled. "Sounds like something my mother would have loved." When Maggie looked at her, Ava added. "You know, the rapture? She was big on that."

And here they were, back in church again. Kenny diffused any response by handing a brush to Ava. "Can you trim around the tub tile? I'll roll when you guys are done with that."

"Sure." She took the brush and put her hand on her stomach. "Yikes, did you hear that? I skipped lunch."

"Are you hungry?" he asked, then turned to Maggie. "Are you? I totally forgot lunch."

"I'm starved," Maggie said. "Martinelli's is the best pizza in Coconut Key, and they deliver. Want me to call and get some?"

"I love pizza," Ava said. "My mom used to try to make it, but it was always a disaster. Remember, Dad?"

He threw a quick look over his shoulder, not sure why she'd bring that up right now. They'd been talking about her, but Maggie brought her up first, so that was different. "Uh, yeah, I do."

"It was shaped like Australia," Ava told Maggie. "Dad called it the Aussie pizza."

"That's cute," Maggie said, her focus on a tricky bit of trim.

"She wasn't much of a cook, but when she did, she always went big," Ava added. "For a while she was in a soufflé stage. Remember, Dad?"

Okay, enough. "I sure do," he said, giving her a look that she didn't see. "Let's definitely call for that pizza now. Martinelli's, is it? I don't think I've had it yet."

"You'll love it. I highly recommend the pineapple and

pepperoni for those adventurous in pizzaville." Maggie put her brush down. "I have the number in my phone. You think one large is enough?"

"Perfect," Kenny said, taking a breath when she left and waiting until her voice floated down the hall before he turned to his daughter. "Ava," he said. "What exactly are you doing?"

"Um...painting this trim? Is it bad?"

"I mean...bringing up Mom in every sentence."

She blinked at him. "Am I not allowed to talk about her, Dad?"

"Of course you can talk about her, but not constantly."

"Or not at all," she fired back. "Is that the way it has to be? We can't acknowledge that she lived and breathed and cooked and was part of our life?" Her voice rose with emotion.

"Shhh. We just have to be respectful."

"Of her?" She pointed toward the hall with her brush. "What about my mother? Can't we be respectful of her? Can't we talk about her and remember her? Maybe Maggie wants to. Maybe she wants to know more about your wife and how much we loved her."

He stared at her for a moment. "Maybe," he said calmly. "We should understand that it might make Maggie uncomfortable to talk about her."

"Or it might make you uncomfortable," she said.

"That's not true. I—"

She shoved the brush in his hand. "Beck was wrong. This was a dumb idea. I'm going back home."

He just stared at her. "Beck? Wrong about what?"

She just shook her head, stepping to the door. "Bye, Dad. Have fun with your new girlfriend trying to act like Mom never existed. Hope that works out for you."

"Ava." He ground out her name, forgetting how frustrating she could be when she turned immature and snotty.

But she bolted into the hall, letting out a gasp. "Oh, sorry."

"Nope, my fault for..." Maggie's voice faded because no doubt she'd heard the whole conversation or enough of it. "Don't leave, Ava."

"I have to. You guys have fun."

"But the pizza is coming."

"With pineapple? No thanks. My mom hated that. She said pineapple on pizza should be illegal. My dad hated it, too, but he won't tell you that."

"Ava." He stepped into the hall just as she shot past Maggie, her hair flying as she ran toward the door in a perfect storm of teenage emotions, hormones, and attitude.

And pain. He couldn't forget she had pain, too.

"It's fine," Maggie said softly when the door slammed. "She's young. And...this is new."

New enough that Ava could wreck the whole thing.

She took the paint brush he held and gave him a tight smile. "For what it's worth, I only put pineapple on half. Never let it be said I can't compromise."

He touched her chin, lifting her face a little. "You know what I want, Maggie?"

"Extra pepperoni?"

"To talk."

"About what?"

"Everything. Nothing. My wife and my life and my kid and...us. I don't know if that's fun and easy enough for you, but you better know that's what I want."

She let out a shuddering sigh. "Okay, Kenny. Let's talk."

CHAPTER SEVEN

BECK

*I*t had been a long time since Beck sneaked off to a man's house as the hour neared midnight. In fact, the last time she did that, she was a teenager and got pregnant.

Well, that wasn't going to happen tonight, she thought with a smile as she drove down a deserted US1. For one thing, she was fifty-six and the man she was meeting was nearing fifty-nine. For another, she and Josh were a long, long way from being that physical. And for a third, she just wanted one more chance to give him support and sympathy for his loss and maybe...a kiss goodbye before he left.

Because that felt right.

At one of the intersections in town, she slowed her car and she glanced to her right, seeing a few lights on at the Sunset Lodge, the small courtyard motel where Bill Dobson was currently staying.

The irony of that wasn't lost on Beck. In fact, she was buried in irony. Because, yes, that very man sleeping in one of those rooms had been the one she'd sneaked out to see that night so many, many years ago. He'd been the boy waiting in a gold Camaro at the end of her street. His engine, and the Camaro's, had been roaring.

A shiver danced over her at the memory, which she'd so long ago put into a lock box.

Any time she'd even thought about that period in her life, she'd always drifted to that morning in the hospital when her mother refused to let her hold a baby that had hurt like hell to deliver. It remained one of the most poignant and impactful memories of her life, and one that had left a hole so deep she hadn't realized it was there.

That hole seemed to be filled now that she'd gotten to know the son she gave up that day. And Ava, of course, a granddaughter she didn't know existed. But Bill Dobson? She'd mostly forgotten about him, except in passing. To her, he was little more than the bad boy from a math class who only liked Beck Mitchell because she was "unattainable."

She'd been social, popular, and outgoing. Beck didn't have anything to do with the kids who cut class and took shop instead of AP English, especially not the boy who frequently had a guitar pick between his teeth.

But he had attained her...with a relentless onslaught of teasing in that math class. Geometry, was it? Maybe algebra. She didn't remember. But she remembered how he always had a faint scent of leather from his jackets and his hair was thick and dark and long. And how he somehow managed to get her phone number. Then she'd get late night whispery calls she'd take on the hall phone so Olivia didn't hear her laugh and know she wasn't talking to a girlfriend.

Finally, Bad Boy Billy wore her down for a date and *that* she couldn't hide.

That memory was crystal clear. It was late in the afternoon when she told Olivia she was going out with him, a boy her mother had met once when he came over to study math. Olivia had turned from the sink where she'd been peeling potatoes and screamed at her.

Beck had been in shock—Olivia Mitchell had been a difficult mother, no question. Judgmental, strict, and cold. But she'd rarely yelled. That day, her voice shook the windows.

And when Beck declared that yes, she *was* going out with Billy Dobson, Olivia slapped her across the face.

She never remembered her mother hitting her before or after that moment.

But now she understood. Olivia had no doubt believed that loose morals were hereditary and Beck, herself a product of a teenage liaison, was bound to drop her panties.

Well, hell. Drop she did. And maybe Olivia was right about those morals because...Savannah. Not a teenager, but still pregnant and not married. Thankfully, it was a different, far less judgmental world.

She slowed when her car reached the shopping strip where Josh's shop was located, instantly seeing his truck. So, Jessie was right; Josh *was* burning the midnight oil finishing that mantle he'd promised a customer before they left in the morning.

The decision to come over here had been impulsive, but it felt right. Something was hanging in the air between them and even if she couldn't tell him the truth about Bill, since she hadn't asked Kenny, she could clear the air a little.

She wanted him to know she'd miss him, she thought as she pulled into the lot and parked next to his truck. And get that kiss.

"It's good to have a goal, Beck," she whispered to herself.

Climbing out, she walked to the door, squinting into the darkened front of the shop. Should she go around back? Should she knock or text him? Should she...not have come?

The latch on the door clicked and opened before she had a chance to decide her course of action.

"Beck?" Josh pushed the glass door wider. "I saw the lights in the lot and...what are you doing here?"

"I wanted to see you again," she said. "And say goodbye."

His brows lifted imperceptibly as he opened the door wider. "I thought we did say goodbye."

"Again," she added on a soft laugh, coming into the cool air-conditioned storefront. "And properly."

He angled his head and fought a half smile. "Huh. Imagine that."

"How are you feeling?"

With a tight smile, he shrugged. "Sad. Mortal. Worried about my sister, and trying to finish this mantle before I pack and leave at dawn. Wanna see it?"

"Yes." She followed him back into his workshop, which felt entirely different at night than it did when daylight was streaming in from the high windows. The only light in here was artificial, a lamp on a stand beaming directly at the mantle laying on a workbench. The rest of the room was dark, shadowy, and cozy from the smell of fresh wood.

"Oh, Josh," she exclaimed as she got closer. "It's stunning."

"I think I saved that old Key West feel that it came with, but I'm happy with the new glossy look."

She ran her fingers along the top of the carved wood, marveling at his talent. "You managed to transform it but save it at the same time. What a skill."

"Thanks." He crossed his arms and leaned back. "I wish I could see the client's face when they pick it up tomorrow, but by the time they get here, Jess and I will be darn near Jacksonville."

"Oh, it's a long trip. I'm glad you're going to stop."

He snorted softly. "Jessie thinks we're going to stop. Once I hit eight hours on the road, what's another three? I want to get there, and I hate stopping."

"I won't tell her," she said.

"Don't. Jessie hates change."

"I know she does." Beck slid onto the leather-topped stool, finally comfortable. Why wouldn't she be, though? This was Josh and they were friends.

But friends didn't always visit friends at eleven-thirty at night.

"You know when she started hating change?" he asked. "When you moved away. She was traumatized by that loss and talked about you incessantly for a solid two years."

And Olivia destroyed Jessie's letters, and never mailed Beck's to her. She made a face, still harboring resentment for the woman. "And then she forgot me, huh?"

"No, then my dad took off with Marilyn Digman and Jessie had a new change in her life to hate."

"How old were you guys?" she asked.

"I was, what? Fourteen, I guess."

"Tender."

"Around the same age as Heather's kids," he said glumly. "I was old enough to be badly bruised. Old enough to vow I'd never leave my wife." He gave her a tight smile. "But then, life does throw curve balls, doesn't it?"

"You didn't leave your wife, did you?" She remembered him telling her they'd grown apart, with completely different ideas of what their life should look like. He wanted simple, she wanted grand. When their kids grew up and moved out, they'd amicably separated.

"Not like my dad did, but I moved away, back here."

"Miami's not that far," she said. "It sounds like your dad really left, and started a new family. That had to hurt."

He shrugged. "My move, my divorce, felt a little like a failure. But, unlike my sister, I *am* a fan of change. And I really liked the slower pace down here and the chance to do something I really loved. Owning a moving company was lucrative, but not my life's passion." He touched one of the carved columns that ran down the side of the mantle, as if to underscore how proud he was of his work.

"But Jessie?" he continued, obviously in a mood to talk and share feelings, no doubt because a family member had just passed. "Opening that restaurant was the biggest change in her life—well, after losing Chuck." He grimaced. "Huge loss, that man. I considered him every bit a brother. I'm kind of reliving it again today, to be honest."

"Jessie is, too," Beck told him. "I've talked to her a few times today and she's so in sync with Heather's loss. And, in some weird way, a little jealous that Heather's getting the closure that Jessie never did, since they didn't find Chuck's body after the boating accident."

Josh grunted softly. "Now those were some dark days."

"I'm so sorry I never got to meet him," Beck said.

"Fortunately, Jessie has you now, and has always had Lovely. But I'm so glad you're here for her, Beck. You two have always been little peas in a pod, even when you were elementary school kids." He grinned. "Annoying as hell, too, as I recall."

"We aimed to annoy."

He laughed at that, then picked up a tool from the bench, slowly replacing it into a rack on the side, silent.

"And I'm here for her, of course," Beck added, suddenly too aware of that silence. "And...you. Whatever you need."

He looked up. "Thanks."

"Peyton's got the restaurant covered, more or less. Do you need anything here? I can stop in while you're gone, pick up packages, or...whatever you need."

"My apprentice, Brody, is here," he said. "But that's really sweet of you, Beck. I know you have your hands full."

She let out a little moan. "I do, and I guess I have to thank you for the latest semi-drama."

He inched back. "What'd I do?"

"Suggested I talk to Ava about Maggie," she told him.

"I did, and you were right. There are issues. I gave her some advice and I don't know if she followed it or not, but she did go over to their rental to help Kenny and Maggie paint. And then she came home, had her face in her phone, barely talked through dinner, took a two-hour walk on the beach, and went back to Lovely's instead of staying and hanging out with Savannah like she usually does."

"Really? That's not like her."

"Not like the girl we've come to love, but I do feel like I took ten teenage-progress steps backwards."

"Eeesh. Well, you'll figure it out. You always do."

She smiled at his confidence, not feeling the same, but she hadn't come here for a pity party over some tension with her granddaughter.

"And you have the reno to keep you busy, too," he added. "Permits will be coming in soon, then demo will start. You'll be up to your eyeballs for a while."

"Oof. Talk about change. And investment. And hope. And, oh, what if the B&B is a flop and I've spent all that money? I'm going to admit I've had a few sleepless nights since Bill showed up with big ideas and...big expenses."

"Did you decide to do the big suite?" He looked surprised, as he would be since they'd just talked about it earlier today. But she had spent an hour with Bill when he got back from Key West with a plan from his architect that was nothing short of dreamy.

"He makes a compelling argument and there is definitely a market for higher-end accommodations all over the Keys. I still haven't signed off on it, though."

"A market for high-end in Coconut Key?" Josh

sounded skeptical and for good reason. This island wasn't known for chic boutique resorts.

"Your sister seemed to think Coconut Key could handle high-end," she said. "Chuck's is a cut above anything else."

"Because that's what Chuck always wanted, as you know. Jessie would probably have been happy running a diner, and it might have been more successful."

She flinched at the truth in that statement. "Tag Jadrien thinks there's an upscale market," she said. "He wants to buy it."

"He wants to impress my sister. And the rest of the world."

"By putting her out of business?" Beck asked.

"I don't know what his game is," he admitted. "I never have."

"Maybe he thinks if she doesn't have her own restaurant, she'll work for him and he can win the girl he lost in high school," she suggested.

"Maybe, but I always get the vibe that the man has an agenda, driving a Tesla and living large like he does."

"I've never met him," Beck said, eyeing Josh as her brain went back to earlier in the conversation. "But you don't like the high-end B&B idea, do you?"

He gave a soft, scoffing laugh. "Beck, it's not my B&B or my money or my future. You're the one who has to take a risk with Dobson...or on his ideas," he added quickly.

"With big risks come big rewards," she said, parroting one of Bill's favorite sayings.

"And big debt."

She narrowed her eyes at him. "You do realize this is

the second time I've been in this studio in the space of one day when we've had the same argument."

"We're having an argument?" He lifted his brows. "I'm having a discussion. You're having...doubts."

She blew out a breath. "You really don't like him, do you?" A little skitter of irritation slid around her chest, which was understandable. Bill was the biological father of her son and whether anyone knew that or not, it made her just a tad bit defensive about the guy.

"Dobson?"

"Bill. His name is Bill, and it's just such a typical guy thing to only call the other one by

his last name as if you can demean him a little that way."

He lifted another tool, silent, his gaze on it while he wiped the blade with a cloth and carefully stored it next to the others.

"If you really want to hurt me," he said softly, "call me typical."

Her heart dropped with the same force as her feet as she slipped off the stool and took a step closer. "Josh. I'm sorry. I didn't come here to fight."

"Then why did you come here?"

She let out a slow exhale. "I realized how much I'll miss you." She took one step closer, rooting for courage to say the absolute truth because he deserved nothing less. "I wanted to tell you that. I wanted to tell you I'm sorry that we didn't take that bachelor auction date." Two more steps. "And I wanted to..." *Kiss you.*

She looked up at him, caught by the undercurrent of strength in his blue eyes.

"Beck," he said softly. "This is all so new to you."

"This...like..." She tapped her chest, then his, then hers again. "This?"

He placed one finger on her lips. "This."

She held his gaze, not moving. "And your point is..."

"You've been single for about two and a half weeks."

Oh. Sucking in a very soft breath, she moved back a centimeter, heat suddenly crawling up her chest. "True. And this is your way of saying you think I'm a rookie who should bide her time, settle down, and not attempt midnight...rendezvous?"

"Is that what this is?" He broke into a slow smile and looked at her. "I think you're the best friend I've had in a long time. I don't want to screw that up."

Okay, this was confusing. "Josh, when you drove me home from the bachelor auction, you were pretty clear that you were ready to take our friendship to the next level. We both agreed—maybe not in writing, but it was clear to me—that when my divorce was final, under the auspices of a date I purchased as a charitable donation, we would...find that level. Right? And earlier today, you tried to set up that date."

He nodded, still looking at her.

"What changed? The fact that you're leaving? Or that my divorce is real now and you..." She swallowed, not willing to believe he was that capricious. "What's different now than six weeks ago when we came home that night?"

"Dobson," he murmured again.

"What? Why?"

He drew back a step. "I don't know," he said, nothing but raw honesty in his voice. "But there's something about that guy that makes me feel there's more to his story than what he's telling us."

Her throat tightened. There *was* more to his story. He was Kenny's father. She'd known him as a teenager. She'd sneaked out that night, lost her virginity in the Camaro, and ended up a teen statistic.

"Like I said," he whispered, finally looking away as if one of those tools was calling his name.

She wasn't following. "What does that mean, 'like I said?'" Could he *know?* Should she tell him?

"It means look at your face when I mention his name. You flush, your eyes dilate, your lips part."

"Oh, for heaven's sake, Josh. You make me sound like I'm walking around in a romance novel." She ground out the words, shame morphing into anger with each one. "That's not like you."

"It's not like *you.*"

"There *is* more to him," she fired back, getting a look of sheer confusion.

"What do you mean? With you two? You're..."

She put her hand on his arm and made a decision that she'd explain to Bill and Kenny later. She owed this man the truth.

"Yeah?" he asked expectantly.

"Josh, Bill Dobson is Kenny's biological father."

His frown deepened as he drew back an inch. "He's..."

"He was my teenage...mistake."

"Are you serious?"

She nodded. "He found Kenny up in Atlanta and they became friends. Great friends. And he was there when Kenny needed him the most, and he's been awesome. But Ava doesn't know. No one does but Lovely, because I'd told her his name once. Kenny is waiting to decide when and how to tell Ava, and I'm letting him."

For a long time, he stared at her, processing the news. "I see the resemblance," he finally said.

"That's it? That's all you have to say?"

"What else is there to say?" he asked. "I mean, other than the obvious. Do you still have feelings for your... teenage mistake?"

She smiled. "None except gratitude that he's been so good to Kenny and Ava. And he came through when I needed a general contractor."

"Okay..." But he sounded a little dubious. "You know, Beck, life's too short to worry about stuff like this. Not that this isn't huge news and potentially...boat rocking, but—"

"It shouldn't rock any boats."

"I hope it doesn't. But when I think about what I'm going to say at my brother-in-law's funeral in a few days, this isn't the end of the world."

He was so right. She reached up and hugged him, only a little disappointed when he pressed his lips on her hair for a quick, platonic kiss on the head.

Well, she had come for a kiss. Just not that kind.

CHAPTER EIGHT

SAVANNAH

*T*he noise was interminable and maddening and not fair to a pregnant woman who had to stay on her back.

There were boots clomping up and down the stairs and drills screaming at an ear-splitting pitch and hammers pounding nails into two-by-fours and men who couldn't speak to each other, they had to yell and snort and curse and *she hated them all.*

"Make it stop!" Savannah took one of the pillows and smashed it over her head, muffling the sound of a house renovation over her head.

With another cranky moan, she threw the pillow next to her, knocking her tablet to the floor and taking the phone with it. The phone that was flashing with an incoming call.

From Nick Frye.

Swearing, she tried to push up—no mean feat for seven months pregnant—and stand, which took a few seconds, then lunged for the phone, snagging it just in time to get the call.

"Just in the nick of time," she whispered, breathless.

"My new name? Nick of Time? It sounds sexy when you say it like that."

She snorted, looking down at the yellow tent-sized T-shirt she wore, bare feet that hadn't seen the inside of a salon in way too long, and then back up to get a glimpse of her hair in the mirror. All she could say was thank God this wasn't FaceTime.

"That's me, sexy and seven weeks from delivery."

"Babe, how ya feelin'?"

Babe. Why did he do that? This one-night stand superstar actor who really shouldn't care about the barista he bedded and impregnated. But he called every day, frequently more than once. His voice was always kind, and the babe thing...somehow that just started.

"I feel..." Some extremely noisy electric tool shrieked. "Overwhelmed," she admitted.

"The baby? Everything okay?" Again, actual *care* in his voice.

"He's fine. Very active. Decided to kickbox my uterus at three in the morning." She managed to settle back on the bed. "No, it's my mother's renovation. Very noisy. Lots of loud men and their power tools."

"Should I be jealous?"

What? "Of that buzzsaw you hear? Nah. I just need to get out of here so bad I literally can't stand it."

"Bed rest, Sav. Doctor's orders."

"I know, I know, but..." She exhaled and eased back onto her mountain of pillows. "I long for a mani-pedi with an endless foot massage, and maybe a day of shopping for clothes that wouldn't double as a sheet, but I don't want to walk. I want to be carried there like Cleopatra on a platform bed surrounded by drapes and purple pillows." When he laughed at that, she added, "A girl can dream, you know."

"Don't you get out in a few days for the next doctor appointment?" he asked, surprising her that he really listened to her schedule. This guy who juggled *People Magazine* interviews with Hollywood parties and important meetings with his agent. He knew when she was going to the doctor? Stunning.

"I do, but it's not quite Cleopatra on the way to a mani-pedi. Enough about that," she said, crossing her ankles and trying to ignore her chipped toes. "How was the big scene today? Twenty takes?"

"Three, and the second two were because they wanted two other angles."

"Wow. Impressive." She closed her eyes and imagined his trailer on the set of *Magic Man,* where he starred in a sometimes dark, sometimes scary, always riveting drama set in Las Vegas, but filmed on a set in L.A. "Is that a wrap for the week?"

"I wish. We have pick-ups all day tomorrow and the press junket continues. Please be sure to watch me on *E! Weekly* or whatever."

"I'd love to. Send me a schedule or have your publicist send it." As soon as she said it, she cringed. "Or not, if you don't want anyone to know we're talking."

"Savannah, why do you say things like that?" The question had just enough hurt in it to make her think he really cared.

"Look, Nick. I'm under no delusions here. You're...

you. Nick Frye. And I'm an unemployed twenty-nine-year-old—for a few more days anyway—currently pregnant and living with my mother. Please."

"You have a birthday coming up?"

See, that's what he did that was maddening and alluring and confusing and wonderful. He heard little things, the type of throw-away comments that most men miss unless you slammed them over the head with it, and he cared.

"Yep, next Thursday. The big three-oh. Yikes."

"I went to Santorini for my thirtieth birthday. Rented the most amazing yacht and cruised all over the Greek islands."

"Just what I was planning to do," she said on a light laugh.

He chuckled. "They have yachts in the Keys."

"Plenty of them, but I'm kind of a skiff girl. Love when they get caught up in a waterspout and my teenage niece has to save me."

"I still think that should be in a movie," he said. "Do you know how close you came to losing our baby?"

Her heart flipped around like that skiff in the water that day. *Our baby.* "Well, this one had a happy ending, my friend. No need to worry. And I do want to know your publicity schedule," she added, softening her voice. "Junior and I will watch on my iPad and I'll tell him all about how famous and handsome his daddy is."

He let out a sound that could have been a soft laugh or a whimper or just...uninterpretable. "When you say things like that, Savannah...it makes me want to turn my life upside down."

And that made her entire stomach turn upside down.

She had to remember the man was an actor, award-winning and believable. For whatever reason, he was digging this "role," but it couldn't last, wouldn't last, and had to end eventually. Didn't it?

"So, two more episodes to film," he said, the words snapping her out of her thoughts.

"That's cool. Do you have another show or movie lined up?" She didn't even know if those were the right words. Hollywood people probably said "another property" or a "gig" or something that only the in-crowd knew.

"I'm taking some time off."

"That'd be nice."

"So I can be there for the birth."

Wait...*what?* "Did you say..." That buzzsaw screamed again, sounding a lot like the forceful "Nooooo!" in her head.

"Savannah, do you really think I'm going to let you go through childbirth alone?"

Yes, she absolutely did. And wasn't at all sure she wanted him there. Giving birth was stressful and messy and painful. She didn't want some hot guy showing up to make her self-conscious. Even if he was the baby daddy.

"Not necessary," she said firmly.

"Not your call."

She sat up a little, irked. "Actually, it is. I know you're the father and you have rights, Nick. I'm patiently waiting to find out which of those rights you'd like to exercise and how. But for the birth? I just want to be with my family. Please."

He was quiet for a long time, the only sound a lone hammer slamming into some poor nail the way his silence was hitting her. Hard.

"Please," she added when it went on way too long.

"Savannah, this isn't about exercising rights." He spoke slowly, as if choosing every word with great care. "This is about the most important day of either one of our lives. Our son is going to be born. A life that we created."

"You make it sound like we were on that yacht in Santorini instead of the W Hotel in Santa Monica across the street from the coffee shop where you picked me up." She groaned at the thought, so mad that fate or the universe or God or who*ever* thought it would be hilarious if her really bad, impulsive, stupid, and reckless decision was forever memorialized with the creation of a human being. "The angels didn't sing, Nick. The earth didn't move."

"Whoa, way to cut me to the core, Sav."

"I mean, please don't elevate this event to something more than it is for you. I appreciate your interest and support and help, but can we be honest about what's happening here?"

"Who's being dishonest?" he asked, undaunted by her argument. "I'm out of my mind with excitement about having a kid, Savannah."

She took a shaky breath. "So, you definitely want to be in his life."

"Of course."

"Like, you are going to want him to live in Los Angeles?"

He didn't answer. In fact, he was so silent, she glanced at the phone, thinking the call dropped.

"Hey, I gotta go," he finally said. "I'll check in later."

"Nick." She tried to swallow, surprised at how tight

her throat was. "I have to know. It's driving me crazy. What are your plans with this kid?"

"I don't have plans, Savannah," he said. "Except I'd really like you to give me a chance."

She frowned. What did that mean?

"Gotta run. Oh, wait. What day is it?"

"Today? Tuesday—"

He laughed. "No, nitwit. Your birthday."

"Oh, the fourteenth."

"Good to know. Bye, babe."

Babe again. "Bye, Nick."

She hung up the phone, only realizing then that her whole body was so tense her muscles actually hurt. The drill was shrieking. The hammer was pounding. The boots were clumping.

It was enough to make a woman cry. Which, damn it, she was.

CHAPTER NINE
PEYTON

*A*s she settled into Jessie's office chair, Peyton blew out a sigh of relief that she had this escape hatch while Coquina House was under construction. Granted, hiding in the back office of a restaurant wasn't ideal, especially because Chuck's seemed really sad and lonely in its current state of "closed for the season."

But the space and quiet had given Peyton exactly what she needed to finish the cookbook galleys and get them ready for one final round of proofing. After that, she'd dive into formatting, a technically challenging process that required a professional.

So, today she'd scheduled a conference call with a book formatter who would create the computer file necessary to take this baby from Peyton's laptop to readers, whether they bought the book for their Kindle or ordered it in print. She just prayed Steve Wallace was taking new clients and could work *Cuisine* into his schedule shortly.

While she waited for their scheduled phone call, she

scrolled through the book pages on her laptop, smiling as she remembered personally cooking every single recipe in the book.

She returned to the front matter, looking at the empty pages still waiting for more. A Dedication, which Jessie said she'd send when she had a chance. No doubt it would be dedicated to Chuck, so writing that would be difficult.

And the book still needed an official Introduction, which had Peyton stymied. Of course, she could write it herself, and not sign a name to it. Then it would just be a garden-variety intro that would tell readers what to expect on the pages ahead.

But great cookbooks usually had someone with some weight in the industry, or a celebrity, pen that essay. She knew a few from other cookbooks, but not well enough to call without having the backing of a New York publishing house. Would Savannah's famous friend, Nick, do it? He seemed pretty willing to do just about anything for her, she thought with a twinge of jealousy.

Not that she was envious...well, maybe she was a little. Savannah was about to have the baby that Peyton longed for, even if she would likely raise it on her own. And who knew? Maybe the superstar actor could be a special someone for Savannah and a good dad to the—

Her phone buzzed and she grabbed it, hoping it was the formatter calling a few minutes early. She glanced at the screen and it was him, but he was texting to say he was running late and needed another hour before he could call her.

She texted back and pushed away from the desk, a little frustrated with an unproductive hour. It reminded her of the job she'd left in New York, which was more downtime and waiting than actual work.

Publishing might be what she always thought she wanted to do, but, except for this passion project of Jessie's cookbook, the whole industry had disappointed her. Her gaze shifted to the computer, landing on Chuck's "Anniversary" Crab Cakes, one of the most popular items on the restaurant's menu and one Peyton never tired of recreating.

She inched closer, re-reading the one paragraph description of the dish, a section she'd written after she'd made the crab cakes with Jessie. While they'd cooked the simple but magnificent patties, Jessie had shared the story of how her late husband had made a tradition of catching fresh crab to make this dish on their anniversary every year. A seasoned and skilled fisherman, Chuck had taken Jessie crabbing the day he'd proposed. After that, he caught fresh crab every year for their anniversary, and they recreated that special night.

She let out a sad sigh. What would it be like to have that kind of love and tradition? Yes, it came with pain. Jessie mourned her husband every day, which was achingly sad. But they'd had so many years of anniversary crab cakes.

Clearing the screen, Peyton stood and headed into the empty, cool kitchen, knowing deep down inside how she wanted to spend this empty hour. She'd fill it by making the crab cakes again, instead of feeling sorry for her single self.

In the freezer, she found a pound of crabmeat, marked and dated in Val Sanchez's handwriting, which didn't help her efforts to cancel the pity party.

She and Val had dated for two months after she moved down here, but then he finally shared his tragic tale of how he'd been engaged, only to lose his fiancée to leukemia right before they could marry. With that revelation, so much about Val became crystal clear.

It turns out he wasn't a joke-slinging fisherman who lived off the sea without a care in the world. Well, he was. But before that, when he'd been happy and in love with his high school sweetheart, he'd been a Miami business accountant with a whole life ahead of him.

When that all changed, he covered his broken heart with silly jokes and puns and hid from his pain by moving to the Keys, away from all his memories, to fish. His MBA from the University of Miami helped him build a steady and strong business with dozens of local restaurants as customers.

But she didn't know any of that while they'd dated for a few months. And once he revealed his sad story, a dam broke. Val decided he had to go back to Miami and face his demons.

"And that was the end of that," Peyton murmured as she headed to the industrial-sized fridge for the rest of the ingredients.

No one had cooked in here for a while, but she was able to find what she needed, softly humming to herself as she lined up her prep bowls, defrosted the crabmeat, and started chopping and mixing.

And suddenly, magically, everything in the world disappeared. As she moved through each step with thought and purpose, she forgot the delayed meeting, the daunting task of promoting the cookbook and saving Chuck's, and even the low-grade ache of missing Val.

Ever since Jessie had handed her a recipe and said, "Make this!" Peyton had tapped into something deep and primal when she was in the kitchen. Lost in the process of following the crab cake recipe she'd actually memorized the second time she made it, she folded the mixture, formed the patties, and fired up her favorite sauté pan to get these babies sizzling to a gorgeous gold.

Just as she was ready to slide the first one out of the pan, a noisy knock at the back door yanked her to reality. Could those vendors not read the sign or listen to the messages she'd sent letting them know Chuck's was on a seasonal break?

Well, she was not leaving these cakes until they were done to perfection, so whoever it was could knock and knock.

She flipped the last one and studied its color, just about to ease it onto the paper towel when she heard the door open, making her gasp. She hadn't locked it, but who would just come in?

Wiping her hands on a towel she stepped to the side of the prep station, coming face to face with a man as he entered unannounced.

And not just any man...but Chef Tag Jadrien, who Peyton considered Public Enemy Number One. If he hadn't opened a restaurant in Coconut Key, Chuck's might still be thriving.

She blinked at the fifty-something man with his shoulder-length hair pulled back into a ponytail, wireless glasses resting on a prominent nose that accented stark cheekbones and a day's worth of scruff.

"Can I help you?"

"Hello. Peyton, is it?"

He remembered her name? She had no recollection of being formally introduced on the two occasions they'd met—once at his main restaurant in Key West when he stopped at their table to talk to Jessie, and another time, about two months ago when he'd come to Chuck's with an offer to buy the restaurant.

"Peyton Foster," she confirmed, wiping her hand again but not offering it in greeting. "Are you in the habit of breaking and entering restaurants, Chef?"

A smile flickered. "Only when the employees leave the door unlocked, their car is out back, and no one answers." He moved into the kitchen with an irritating sense of entitlement and a noisy inhale.

He was an intimidating man for sure, but it helped that Peyton knew his real name was Taggert Lutwack and that he'd been a shy, awkward teenager who'd lost Jessie to Chuck when they were in high school.

Good heavens, the man had truly managed to transform awkward into arrogant. That was some cooking school he went to.

"Jessie's not here," she said.

He gave her a sad look. "I heard about her brother-in-law. How's the family doing?"

"How do you know about Drew?"

"Because the restaurant industry in general and Coconut Key in particular are very, very small and gossipy. Is she doing okay?"

"Hanging in there, I suppose."

He nodded and came closer to the prep counter. "I thought I smelled Anniversary Crab Cakes." He leaned over the paper towel, using his hand to wave the aroma toward his nose. "Perfect amount of garlic, too." He gestured toward one to pick it up. "May I?"

No. She swallowed the word, too stunned to let it out, watching in shocked silence as he lifted one of the crab cakes, inhaled the scent again, then closed his eyes and put the whole darn thing right into his mouth.

"Oh my God," he said as he chewed, his eyes closing in what could only be described as ecstasy. "You have a gift."

"No, I have a great recipe. That's Jessie's gift."

He chewed and swallowed, eyes fully closed as he seemed to somehow interpret the bite.

"Worcester, yes, which is in any respectable crab cake, but you layered the flavor." Finally he opened his eyes and looked at her. "Oh, and lime? Genius move. Where did you study?"

She bit back a soft laugh. "In this kitchen. On YouTube and the Food Network. Please, don't try and flatter me, Chef. I'm seriously a rookie. Cooking is a hobby and part time job and I'm just following Chef Jessie's recipe."

"I refuse to believe that."

"Believe what you want, but it's true."

"No one has ever trained you?"

She considered how to answer that. "I started with Jessie's recipes which are not only incredibly easy and fun to follow, they made me feel...confident."

"I can taste that confidence," he said. "It's as subtle but important as the lime."

She almost smiled. Could he be for real? "That's all Jessie," she said. "That's her gift as a chef. Not just her ability to, what did you say? Layer flavors? But also the fact that recreating her recipes makes the cook feel...empowered."

"Brilliant," he said.

She responded with a tight smile. "So, can you tell me exactly what it is you're doing here? Because we're closed and I'm alone, and, frankly, I'm not comfortable."

"Oh, sorry. I don't mean to make you uncomfortable." He took a step back as if to underscore that.

"Then you shouldn't have walked right in like you own the place."

"Yet." He grinned, which really didn't soften the annoyance of that response. "I saw a car in the lot and took a chance."

"A chance on what?"

His eyes flickered like he was trying to think of the right thing to say, but then he cast his gaze down on the crab cakes. "You really should make the move from hobbyist to professional. Have you ever considered that?"

"Because I can make a decent crab cake? Not really." Although, truth be told, she had played with the idea in her head. It didn't seem like a super viable career plan, but then, with publishing behind her, maybe it could be. "A chance on what?" she repeated.

He sighed, then said, "I came to ask you what it would take to get Jessica to say yes to my offer."

Really? First of all, something about the way he said it made her doubt that it was true. And second, the request was rude and inappropriate. "I have no idea how to answer that," she said. "Her business and your offer are private."

"She needs to accept the offer, Peyton," he said, his voice lowering just a note to make it sound extremely serious. "I do not want to put her out of business. I want to save her."

"By buying her dream?" She snorted. "There's got to be a better way."

"Then name it. I want to help her."

She searched his face, ready to dismiss everything he was saying, but something stopped her. He looked... genuine. Serious, even.

"Maybe she's told you we have a history, or maybe she hasn't. But the fact is, I've always..." He hesitated, clearly not sure how much to share. "I want to help her, pure and simple. She means a lot to me, and I..." For the first time, he seemed to be at a loss for words. "I really want to help her, and I'm worried she's in over her head," he finished softly.

Was it possible he was telling the truth? Not just trying to snag one of the best properties on Coconut Key for himself?

So, how could he help her? How could he help Chuck's succeed?

"I have an idea," she said the words slowly, but the idea wasn't hitting her slowly at all. Nope, it was taking shape and slamming her over the head with its rightness.

"You do?"

"If you're serious, then, yes, I have a way you can help her." And if he agreed, then she'd believe him.

"Anything. Just tell me what it is."

She blew out a breath. "Write the Introduction to her upcoming cookbook."

His brows lifted. "Done. Anything else?"

"Really?" She worked to keep her reaction off her face, but failed.

"Of course." Did he realize that the cookbook was to promote the restaurant? He'd have to know that. "I love that idea," he added. "I'd be honored to write the intro. I already know what I'll say."

"Which is..."

"If I tell you, I'll spoil the surprise. You'll have to trust me."

"It seems I just did."

He gave the most natural smile she'd seen from him yet and extended his hand. "I'll have it done in a few days."

Wow. Seriously? This was a major coup. A major coup to legitimize that cookbook. And a major coup that Jessie might not be so thrilled about, but still. *Major.*

"Anything else?" he asked.

"Yes. Next time let *me* open the door."

"Deal." He popped another crab cake in his mouth and left.

Peyton stood in stunned disbelief, not moving until she heard her phone ring with the call from the formatter that she'd been waiting for.

CHAPTER TEN
KENNY

*K*enny used all his strength to tear back the carpet from the second-floor bedroom, swearing softly when it barely budged. Next to him, Bill wasn't helping like he normally did, but instead kneeled next to Kenny, his face stuck in his phone, a few choice words of his own dropping out occasionally.

"Everything okay?" Kenny asked, eyeing the other man who seemed more preoccupied than usual today. Bill was normally the most hands-on contractor Kenny had ever worked with, always eager to get down and dirty with the subs on any job. For the most part on this job, Bill had helped with some of the demo they could do while waiting for permitting, but not today.

"Yeah, yeah, it's fine," he answered gruffly, then exhaled. "Just the usual garbage."

The "usual garbage" generally meant money, paying the trades, and juggling bank draws from various projects. That sort of thing didn't trouble Bill too much, so Kenny wondered if it was something else.

"You need to file that last permit for the third floor, don't you?"

"Yeah, as soon as Beck makes a final decision. But..." Distracted again, he tapped his screen.

"Got a fire in Atlanta you need to put out?" Kenny asked. "Because I can cover everything for the time being." The fact was, Kenny could do the prep work until the subs came in. And even when they did, he could handle anything that came up or call Bill with questions.

There was no reason for him to hang out in a motel and help with this job. But here he was, hanging and helping. And Kenny couldn't help wondering why.

"Nah, I'm okay." Bill stuck his phone in his back pocket, returning his attention to the carpet. "So, how's Maggie?"

"I guess she's fine. Why?"

"Because I like her. I like you and her. Seems like a good match."

He snorted. "Then tell Ava."

"I haven't seen much of Ava lately."

"That makes two of us. I think she's ticked off at me for seeing someone and using the fact that she's temporarily living with Lovely while we do this reno as an excuse to avoid me."

Bill leaned back again, looking at his phone after it vibrated, then he shoved it back in his pocket. "So, what's going on? She doesn't like Maggie?"

"The only time we have all been together, all she did was—"

Bill interrupted him with a grunt, then whipped the phone out again. "Come on, pal. Leave it alone."

"Who's that?"

"Just some BS. I'll be right back. I have to take this." He stepped into the hall, answering the phone with a gruff *hello*. After a long silence, he started talking, too low for Kenny to hear the conversation, which in and of itself was strange. But then he heard Bill's footsteps down the stairs as if he needed privacy and a few minutes later, Beck came into the bedroom.

"Carpet's coming up, huh?" she asked, then laughed. "Talk about stating the obvious."

"You're okay with that, right? That's what we had on the schedule."

"It's okay," she said. "We're making due on bedrooms as long as Ava's comfy at Lovely's house."

"Too comfy, I think. Bill and I were just talking about how we never see her anymore."

"Between Lovely and Savannah, she's being kept busy. And I couldn't be more grateful since all my focus in on the house. Please tell me the hardwood under that carpet is salvageable."

He'd only revealed about a foot or so, but so far so good. "I think you can keep these floors, Beck." But he didn't want the conversation to go back to the house yet. "So is my daughter happy? You seem to be more in touch with her than I am."

"She's having a blast with Lovely," Beck assured him. "The two of them stay up until all hours watching old movies, eating popcorn on the bed with the dogs."

The image gave his chest a little punch of regret for missing that moment with her, but relief, too, that she was enjoying herself. Old movies on the bed with popcorn was so...Elise. In that regard, he was happy for Ava.

"Do you think this room will be uninhabitable for long?"

"I wouldn't plan on anyone sleeping here soon. Are things too crowded?" he asked, mentally skimming the house residents and the rooms. Beck was staying with Peyton in the attic, which they hadn't touched yet, and Savannah was on the first floor. That left two rooms on this floor, one of which was his, at least temporarily.

"Oh, I know, and we're fine. Peyton and I are a little crowded up in the attic, but she says she'll start looking for a place after the baby's born. She thinks she and Savannah should live in a three-bedroom townhouse, but that might be a recipe for World War III."

"Really? They seem to get along great."

"They do," she agreed. "But they used to nearly kill each other as kids. I don't think either one of them wants to commit to anything just yet, but they will. Assuming Savannah stays. We didn't call her 'Tumbleweed' for nothing."

"Well, you know I'm out of your hair in a week when the rental is finally ours. In fact, I'm leaving on Friday to go up to Atlanta and pack the rest of our stuff and haul it down here over the weekend. We should be able to move in on Monday."

"I heard you painted the bathrooms of the new place," she said. "Why can't the landlord let you move in early? Obviously his other tenants are gone."

"He had one last renter lined up ages ago that he couldn't cancel," Kenny explained. "We can get in right after that, and we have a one-year lease."

She let out a soft sigh. "I can't believe it, Kenny. I'm

still pinching myself that you and Ava are staying. No second-guessing that decision, right?"

"Not so far," he said. "As you know, this was all for Ava, who is happier than she's been in years."

"And you're happy?" she asked. When he looked up at her, she shrugged. "Hey, asking that is a mother's prerogative, even if I didn't raise you."

"Fair enough." He looked back down at the carpet for a moment, knowing exactly what he wanted to talk to her about. He'd almost broached the subject with Bill, so clearly he wanted some advice. He couldn't talk to Maggie about it, so he really should take advantage of Beck's genuine interest in his happiness. "There is one thing bugging me."

"What's that?" She lowered herself to the floor, gracefully settling in for maybe more of an actual chat than he wanted to have. "I'm delighted to help with anything."

"I don't know if you know I had a little...tiff with Ava about a week ago," he said. "Did she mention it?"

"Not in any specifics, but I could tell she was unhappy."

"She came over to paint with Maggie and me and..." He lifted a shoulder. "It just didn't go too well. I think she's kind of on the fence about me seeing someone."

"I might be partially to blame, Kenny. I advised her to go over there and get to know Maggie."

"I thought you might have, because that day when she came over, she said, 'Beck was wrong,' and I've been wondering about it ever since."

"Oh, dear. What happened?"

"She just went on a...rant? Rampage? I don't know. She kept bringing every subject back to Elise, which was uncomfortable for everyone. I reprimanded her when Maggie left the room and, wham. That was the last father-daughter moment we've had in a while."

"Oh, Kenny, that *was* my fault," Beck admitted. "She told me she's worried her mother will be forgotten since you have a new woman in your life. I told her that it's fine to talk about Elise, that she should, and that I bet Maggie wanted to hear about her."

"She does," he said. "But Ava came at the process like a bulldozer."

"Because it's so important to her that you keep her mother's memory alive. I don't think she has an issue with you seeing Maggie, but I know she has a very big fear that you are going to forget Elise completely."

He closed his eyes. "I can assure you *that* will never happen."

"It's not me you need to assure," she said, her gentle voice reminding him very much of his mother. His other mother.

"Gotcha. I'll talk to her."

"Good plan. And can I ask you a question that I have no right to ask?"

"Like I could stop you," he said on a laugh. "Hit me."

"Is Maggie a serious relationship? Or is that none of my business?"

"Noneya," he joked. "That's what Elise used to say to me. Noneya...business. But, yeah, it can be your business. I don't care. I like her. She's a great woman, fun and smart and easy to be with."

"And gorgeous."

He gave a soft laugh. "She is. Way too early to tell

where it's going, but I guess I need to know that sooner rather than later."

"Because of Ava?" she guessed.

"Yep. I don't want to see someone casually and set Ava up for a relationship with my 'girlfriend' only to have it end." He shook his head. "Dating is different when you have kids."

"It is," she agreed. "Do you think you'll have a chance to talk to Ava when you go up to pack your house next weekend?"

He threw her a look. "I was kind of thinking Maggie would go with me. She liked the idea of a road trip, but I suppose the three of us could go together." Not what he or Maggie had in mind, but surely she hadn't said yes to the Atlanta trip only because she wanted an overnight or two. Would she mind Ava coming? "Could be a long trip if they're not getting along, though."

"Well, if it isn't a nice little family reunion." Bill blew into the room, the comment making Kenny just close his eyes, never sure how to respond when he made jokes like that. "Hello, there, beautiful Beck. How are you this morning?"

And he never knew how to take it when Bill flirted with Beck. Maybe it was because he knew the history that no one else did, but it always made something protective rise up in Kenny, as if he didn't want her to feel awkward or embarrassed.

Though, to be fair, Beck laughed a lot with him, and didn't seem to mind the attention, so who was he to say?

In fact, she easily took Bill's hand when he offered it, bringing her to a stand.

"I'm fantastic," she said. "But we need to talk a little bit more about that estimate on the upstairs."

"Still not sure, Beck?" Bill asked.

"I don't know. I have to admit it's a little painful to spend that much and lose one whole room. Do you guys still think I'm doing the right thing?"

She said "you guys," so she was asking Kenny, which put him in yet another awkward position with these two. Yanking at more carpet, he considered all the ways to answer her question, while Bill, of course, gushed about how profitable the move would be.

Profitable for Bill, absolutely. For Beck as the owner of the B&B trying to make a living from it? He wasn't sure. Maybe Bill was right about how much a "grand suite" could bring in, but maybe he didn't know squat about Keys rentals.

"Did you and Lovely thoroughly research the comps?" Kenny asked.

"I couldn't find a lot of 'grand' places in Coconut Key," she said. "There's a huge house on the market on the Keys side called The Haven and they're asking over two million, and it's been sitting on the market for a while."

"But that's a house for sale, not a B&B," Bill said.

"With five bedrooms and a guest house, it's big enough to be, and I think it tells you something about the market," Beck replied. "I just don't know if this particular island attracts the big money like, say, Key West. And once I invest the money, I can't undo it. I can't go in and add that second room and bathroom, as I'd originally envisioned. It's a big risk."

Bill put a far-too-friendly arm around her. "Please tell me you're not afraid of risk."

"I'm afraid of spending money on a white elephant that I can't rent or that I take as a loss."

"Rebecca," he said on a slow sigh, tugging her closer. "Come on. Let's go look again. Let's walk around the attic and imagine that you have a suite unlike any other on this island."

"If that's a good thing," she added, throwing a look over her shoulder at Kenny as Bill guided her out of the room toward the third-floor stairs, in full "sales" mode.

The thing was, he didn't have to be in sales mode with her, did he? Wasn't this a favor? Sure, he didn't work for free and no one expected him to, but Beck was essentially family. Hell, not essentially.

They were his *parents*.

Shaking his head at the thought, he felt his phone hum and couldn't help how much he hoped it was Maggie. Sadly, it was an Atlanta number he didn't recognize. He answered it before it went into voice mail, suspecting it was about the move he was arranging.

"Hello?"

"Uh, is this Ken Gallagher?"

"Sure is. How can I help you?"

"Do you still work for Dobson Contracting?"

Did he? Technically? This was probably his last job for Bill's company and, God willing, he'd have his own contractor's license soon, but not yet.

"I do," he confirmed.

"I'm trying to locate Bill. I understand you're a good friend of his."

He could still hear Bill's booming voice as he waxed on about the grand suite, walking Beck up the stairs. But something about the strange call put him on alert.

"I am. Can I get a message to him?"

"Is he in Atlanta? No one seems to be able to find him."

Kenny inched the phone back to glance at the number of the unknown caller again. "Can I ask who's calling?"

"Is he in Atlanta or..." The guy's voice trailed off. "Has he bolted?"

Bolted? "I'm happy to give him a message that you want to talk to him. Should he use this number to reach you?"

"He knows I'm trying to reach him. Maybe you can give him a little nudge."

Why wouldn't Bill return someone's call? "Sure. What's your name?"

"Just tell him Granger doesn't like waiting and the clock is ticking."

What the hell did that mean? But the call disconnected, leaving Kenny holding the phone with a scowl on his face and an unsettled feeling in his chest.

He pushed up and headed toward the stairs, climbing them as he replayed the brief and strange conversation in his head. Bolted? Was that the word the guy used? And who was Granger? Bill didn't work with a sub, trade, or vendor Kenny didn't know, and he'd never heard of Granger. And what did that mean...*the clock is ticking.*

Whoever this was, no wonder Bill didn't want to do business with him.

As he reached the top of the stairs, he heard Beck laughing softly.

"You need to stop it," she said, the playfulness in her voice making Kenny slow his step so he didn't...intrude.

"I can't help it, Beck. Every time I look at you, I think about it."

"I was forty years younger, Bill. And so were you."

"Frost on the roof, fire in the engine...or whatever the saying is."

Whatever it was, it made Beck laugh. "The furnace, I think."

"Somewhere down low."

As Ava would say...*ew*.

Not that he had an issue with Bill seeing a woman—he'd been through the wringer with Natalie, and a woman would be good for him. And Beck was obviously an adult and recently divorced, so what was a little flirtation? Still, they were his parents...and *the Camaro*.

Eesh. He could never look at that muscle car again and not think about...his conception.

The whole thing, like the call, was just weird.

"So, yes or no?" Bill said. "We can do nothing but talk about the project and I'll do my best to persuade you to say yes."

"To what?" she asked on a laugh.

Kenny just closed his eyes and turned around, silently heading back down to the second floor. He'd talk to Bill about the call later. Let them...flirt. He didn't have to witness it.

CHAPTER ELEVEN
BECK

"Come here, now, Rebecca." Bill took her hand and eased her right in front of the attic wall, getting behind her. Not close enough to touch or push the boundaries, but she could sense the warmth of him as he started to talk. "Close your eyes."

"That's not necessary."

"Close 'em," he said. When she did, he added, "Real tight." His head got a tiny bit closer, so that she could feel his breath on her hair. "No cheating."

"Bill, I'm standing in front of a blank wall. I can't *cheat*." But the word echoed in her head.

Was she cheating? She had nothing formal with Josh, nothing but a friendship. They had acknowledged that. They'd also acknowledged that he was a little bit jealous of Bill, so what would Josh think if he walked into this room right now?

She squeezed her eyes tighter to get that image out of her head.

"Now, imagine this entire wall is glass. Floor to ceiling, wall to wall."

"I know you want to put sliders here to capture the view, but—"

"Not just sliders, Rebecca. Glass everywhere."

"Great for hurricanes," she joked.

"Great for charging top dollar, Beck. Water and sky as far as the eye can see. Blue. Green. Dolphins. Sand and surf and sunsets."

She chuckled softly. "We don't have surf in the Keys and we're facing east. You know that, don't you?"

"Work with me here," he continued, undaunted. "We're going to bring the outside in. With the colors and design and so much light. But at night...a fireplace."

How did he manage to make everything sound provocative? Was that because he was selling her an idea for a house...or something else? "Well, for one thing, there isn't a fireplace in this room."

"There could be, quite easily. A gorgeous gas fireplace or even electric." He waited a beat. "Your contractor can do anything, and you need to remember that."

"Well, a fireplace isn't a real high demand amenity in the Keys," she said. "I think my clientele will be more interested in taking the skiff fishing or kayaking down the canals. Maybe shelling and snorkeling."

"You need to think of a *honeymoon suite*, Beck." He crooned the words in her ear, making them sound downright seductive, the way a honeymoon ought to be. "This is going to be a suite for romance."

A shiver she did not want him to notice danced through her body, making her step away from his magnetic hold and back up.

"I love the concept," she said. "But I also think I'll have more families who might want to put the kids in one room and take the other for themselves."

"Put the kids on the second floor. Let Mom and Dad play in the grand suite." He crossed his arms and peered down at her. "Trust me, they'll pay for the privilege and you'll be so glad you made the investment."

She studied his face for a moment, trying to see past the handsome features with the ideal amount of laugh lines and a bit of salt and pepper scruff, to really find the man inside. "Why is it so important to you, Bill? What difference does it make how I set this third floor up?"

"Because I want you to succeed," he replied without a second of hesitation. "I want to play a role in Coquina House being the ultimate B&B destination on Coconut Key."

It was going to be a sweet, warm, comforting place to stay, not the "ultimate" anything, but that wasn't what was bothering her. "Why does it matter to you?"

His broad shoulders sank ever so slightly. "Is it impossible for you to imagine I care about you? The mother of my oldest child?"

"Yes," she answered on an easy laugh, backing another inch away from his overwhelming presence. "We haven't spoken for forty years and I doubt you've given me much more thought than I've given you."

He looked hurt. "Well, that's sad. I've given you a lot of thought. I was the one who found Kenny, you know that. I thought about him plenty over the years, especially after I had my own kids."

She nodded. "And I'm surprised you haven't told

them, since they were the ones who did the DNA tests. Are you going to?"

"The kids would be fine, but..." He looked away. "I was the one who wanted to meet him when I saw those DNA results. I always wanted to know what happened to him. I regretted signing that paper the minute I put my name on it."

"I don't remember you acting regretful," she said. "I remember you being uncomfortable as hell in your parents' living room that day."

"Well, I was a kid myself and about to get that car taken away, so..."

"They weren't mad. They were shocked and disappointed and—"

"Scared of your mother. Your first mother," he corrected. "I don't think Lovely would have scared them. But Olivia?" He cringed. "Scary stuff."

She had been harsh that day. Furious. A little terrifying, honestly. But all because she thought Beck was "like mother like daughter."

"I can't tell you how many times I've thought about how different life would have been if Lovely had raised me instead of giving me to her older sister." She shook her head, still not quite able to comprehend how their decision had entirely changed her life. "For one thing, she'd have never had me give up Kenny for adoption."

"No? You'd have kept him? At sixteen?"

"Lovely had been through it herself and you can tell she's just a much more lenient and, sadly, a more loving, person than Olivia Mitchell. No, we'd have brought that boy up in love and laughter and acrylic paint, swinging on the hammock and running down the beach." It made her a little sad just to think about it. "And if I know her, she'd have offered you whatever role you and your parents wanted in his life."

"But I was in Atlanta."

"And Lovely was here, so..." She laughed, realizing her mistake. "We would never have met."

"And Kenny wouldn't exist. Or Ava." His whole expression softened. "Amazing, isn't it, how things work? That kid was meant to be. They all are."

"Tell me about your other kids, Bill."

He studied her for a minute as if were considering where to start, then he shook his head. "Not here, not now. Let me take you to dinner, Beck. The offer still stands."

Dinner would be a date, and that would feel...wrong. "I'd rather we kept this strictly professional, Bill."

"Gotcha. So, I have a better idea."

"Why do I think this is going to be a workaround that's still a date but isn't called one?" she asked on a soft laugh.

"Because I'm brilliant like that. Listen, I agree, professional. And we have a huge professional decision to make together."

"To grand suite or not to grand suite," she replied.

"Exactly. So why don't we pick a day and research the heck out of it? We'll drive up and down the Keys, visit B&Bs, inns, boutique hotels, and anywhere that you would consider your competition for customers. Let's see what they have and what they charge. I'd like to tour that two-million-dollar mansion you mentioned, too, for the hell of it. Might get some great ideas."

"That's smart," she agreed. "I've only looked online."

"Not the same," he said, and she knew he was right. "You want to see, feel, and smell the places. If you get a list of places together, I'll do the driving and then, the talking. We'll make a day of it. A very professional day," he added. "Afterwards, you can make your final decision."

That sounded fair and safe and...kind of fun.

"I like that plan," she said. "Let's do that sometime in the next few days. Just not Thursday, because that's Savannah's birthday and I wanted to plan something for her."

"Friday, then? Kenny's going up to Atlanta for the weekend and I'm sure we'll hit a freezing point without the permits. It'll be a great day for research."

"Perfect."

"It will be."

She was just a little bit afraid that it might be. Because if time with him was perfect...where did that leave Josh?

She didn't know. But she knew where it left her. Confused.

"WELCOME TO THE GIRLS' hangout club." Savannah waved Beck into her room a few hours later. "Where women are hormonal and the men are not welcome. Except for you, Basil," she added, stroking Lovely's Jack Russell terrier curled next to her. "He has decided his job du jour is to make me feel good, so he can stay."

Beck chuckled as she entered her "old" room as she thought of the suite, smiling at how Savannah had managed to take over the space and make it hers. It looked the same, but felt happy, messy, lived in, and bathed in sunshine.

"You're hormonal?" she asked Lovely, who was resting with Sugar on the recliner they'd brought in from the living room to accommodate Savannah's many guests.

"By association." Lovely pointed to Ava. "This one has PMS." Then to Savannah. "That one has too much baby juice—her words, not mine."

"Somehow I knew that."

"So we're just hanging around discussing the state of our chipped toenails," Savannah told her.

"Sounds riveting."

"Fortunately, I can't see mine and I refuse to let sweet little Ava paint them because I'm a snob and want a proper pedi. But I cannot move this mountain, and Chi-Chi's House of Nails—" She shot a look to Ava. "No, I'm not making that up. That's what it's called. Chi-Chi doesn't make house calls."

"You should let Ava give you a pedicure."

"I'll wait."

Beck settled on the bottom of the bed when Ava rolled to make room for her, letting Beck stroke her long, multi-colored hair that spread over the comforter. "PMS, Ava? How's that going for you?"

"Ask the empty bag of Lay's, this lovely zit the size of Mount Rushmore, or my unbuttoned shorts because I popped out of them."

Beck laughed and looked at Savannah, who leaned against the headboard with a smug expression, hand on belly. "What can I say? The kid's a quick understudy in the wit department. Hormones make us funny, right, grasshopper?"

"Oink."

"Grasshoppers go oink?" Beck asked.

"No, but anyone who ate all those potato chips does." Ava turned over with a moan. "And now I want chocolate!"

Beck smiled at her. "Be happy you're being indulged. Olivia used to tell me PMS was entirely in my head, a manufactured construct to suppress women."

"My sister," Lovely mused. "A woman with no heart."

"Or ovaries, apparently," Savannah said.

"And she fancied herself a feminist," Beck said. "A single mom before it was cool."

"Oh? It's cool?" Savannah grinned. "'Cause it doesn't feel so cool."

Beck studied her daughter for a moment, wondering if she did not *want* to be a single mom. Hard to imagine, since she was so independent, but even surrounded by love and family, she guessed part of Savannah wanted a man— *the* man?—next to her at this time in her life.

"How go the reno wars, Mom?" Savannah asked. "Lovely said you've hit a standstill."

"We have," she said, thinking of her last few hours. "We've stripped or demo'd almost everything we can without the permits. Now we're on hold for some of the trades, too. Kenny's going to drive up to Atlanta on Friday morning and pack up the rest of your stuff."

"Where he wants me to go...with him and Maggie." Ava grunted. "Kill me now."

He'd talked to her about that already? And she didn't like the idea? "Ava." Beck had enough sternness in her voice for Ava's eyes to pop open and look at her.

"What?" she asked, feigning innocence. "It's a long trip."

"You don't want to pack your stuff and say goodbye to your friends?" Beck asked.

"Yeah, I do, but *she's* coming."

"Ava." Beck sliced her with a look.

"I tried to talk to her, but it didn't go so great. It's not that she doesn't want to talk about my mom, it's my dad. He doesn't want anyone to even mention her." Her throat thickened like she might cry. "And he just basically shut me up when I tried." Then her voice rose. "I hate that he just wants her to be forgotten." And then she crumbled as the first tears fell.

"Attention. We have an estrogen spill in aisle four," Savannah said, making them all laugh, even Ava. "Clean up in aisle four."

"I'll clean up," Beck said, reaching to dry one of Ava's tears. "Honey, you and your dad need to have a talk about this. And you need to keep trying with Maggie because I think he really likes her."

She curled her lip.

"So I think you should go with him and Maggie on the trip to Atlanta," Beck continued in her best Mom voice. "It would be a great chance for you to show her a little bit of your old life, maybe introduce her to your friends when you see them. You are going to see your friends, right?"

She nodded, tears threatening again. "I'm going to miss them so much."

Lovely pushed up. "I'll get the chocolate. There's a bar of Godiva in the kitchen."

"Now that's the mother you want during a PMS meltdown," Beck said, giving Lovely her warmest smile. "Thanks." She stroked Ava's hair again. "No gin rummy today?"

"We were talking about boys," Savannah said.

"Oh? Is there a boy?" she asked Ava.

"My boy," Savannah replied. "Nick Frye."

"I've been googling him." Ava popped up, blues forgotten. "Do you know how famous he is, Beck?"

"I do," she said. "He's good-looking and wealthy and famous."

"Listen to how thrilled my mother sounds." Savannah rolled her eyes.

"Well, he's kind of an unknown quantity, honey."

"Except for the five hundred million pages and pictures about him on the internet," Ava said. "He's actually the opposite of unknown."

"Unknown for me, she means," Savannah explained. "And for..." She tapped her belly. "Large beast who likes to kick. Would Kangaroo be a good name for him?"

"They hop, not kick," Ava said.

"Killjoy."

"That's not a good name," Ava said, horrified.

"I meant you."

"How about a real name?" Beck suggested. "Have you whittled that list down to less than fifty? I admit I'm in love with Eli. Such a strong name."

"And biblical," Ava chimed in, getting a surprised look from Beck and Savannah. "My mom read me the Bible," she said, her lower lip starting to slip out. "I liked when she did that."

"Hey, no more tears," Savannah said, using a Mom Voice of her own. "I'll read you the Bible."

"You will?"

"No, but if you cry again, I'll start wailing, too."

"Enough, you two," Beck said gently, getting a little flash of déjà vu from when her girls were little. "Back to the name, Savannah."

"I like Eli, but not with...Frye. Too much rhyme."

"Frye?" Beck blinked at her. "His last name would be Foster, wouldn't it?"

"I don't know because Papa Bear won't say what he wants to do, but he does say that he has an opinion on the name." She dropped her head back with a moan. "Oh, this 'long distance and we don't know each other at all but we're co-parenting' kind of relationship is so difficult."

Ava pointed to the phone on the bed, lighting up. "He's calling," she said.

"Oh, God." Savannah looked at the phone like it was possessed. "Why did I ever tell him about this child?"

"Uh, because he's the father?" Beck reminded her.

Savannah picked up the phone and stared at it. "He's so...into it. And me."

"And that's a bad thing?" Beck asked.

"Right?" Ava chimed in, obviously not shy about having an opinion on this topic.

"It's a...weird thing. And maybe bad. I don't know." Savannah's voice rose like Ava's had. "I need chocolate, too."

"Answer the phone, honey," Beck said calmly. "And be glad he's into you."

"It's like he wants me to believe him or trust him or something."

"Mmmm," Beck said, swallowing her real response

which was...*well, you did sleep with him.* But sometimes the best Mom Voice was a silent one.

Savannah tapped the phone. "Hello, Mr. Frye."

Listening, she looked from Beck to Ava, making a face like it was all just too much for her.

"Excuse me?" she said. "*Why?*"

When her voice went up, Basil's ears perked, as if alerted to a problem. Beck and Ava looked at each other, as intrigued as the dog, while Savannah listened to whatever her famous movie-star baby daddy was saying.

"A secret? I don't like those," she said. "Or surprises," she added. "I'm walking around growing a surprise and a secret, if you recall." Then after a moment, she sighed. "Okay. Fine. You win. Hold on." She held the phone out to Beck. "He wants to talk to you."

"To me?"

"Ridiculous, but here he is, insisting on talking to my mother."

Beck shrugged and took the phone, maybe a wee bit nervous to talk to a celebrity. "Hello...Nick. This is Beck Foster."

"Hey, Beck. Could you leave the room so you and I can have a private discussion without Savannah hearing any of it?"

She felt her eyes widen. "Okay, sure. Hang on." She pushed off the bed and notched her head to the door with a look of confusion.

"Stay here!" Savannah mouthed.

"I'm planning something for her birthday and need your help," Nick said very softly in Beck's ear.

And that was enough for Beck to leave, despite Savannah's choking protests.

"All right," she said as she walked through the living room and kitchen, stepping out on the veranda. "I'm in a private place."

"First of all, it's nice to meet you," he said, his voice so low and pleasant, she had to smile.

"And you, Nick." She took a little breath, getting her bearings with this awkward conversation. "I've heard..." *Next to nothing.* "...about you."

He gave a soft, somewhat self-deprecating laugh that kind of made her instantly like him. "I can only imagine," he said. "But I'm doing my best, Mrs. Foster. Deadbeat isn't in my vocabulary and I'm...charmed by your daughter."

"She is charming."

"And I want to help her celebrate her thirtieth birthday coming up."

"That's very sweet, but unless you're sending a pillow, blanket, or a carton of Pellegrino, she really can't do much celebrating."

"I think she might want more than that. Any ideas?"

"If you can send someone to do a pedicure, she'll be your fan for life." Which might be a little like bringing sand to the beach, considering this man already had millions of fans for life.

"Really?" he said. "Oh, that helps. That helps a lot."

A pedicure? She'd like that. It was sweet. "Is there anything you need me to do?" she asked.

"Well, if it's possible, can you be there on her birthday? And Peyton and Ava. Lovely, of course. Oh, and Savannah's new brother, Ken, is it? And his girlfriend."

Her jaw nearly hit the veranda floor. He knew all their names? Her smile grew. "Sure." He probably wanted to give pedicures for all of them. Must be nice to have big money to throw around. "I guess so, sure. I can get everyone here. How long would you need us?"

"Oh, all day. We'll start at nine. Be at your place—Coquina House, right? I know that's the name of the property, but I don't have an address."

The property. Did he imagine her four-bedroom beach house was a "property" like in L.A.? "It's 143 Coquina Court," she said. "In Coconut Key."

"Coconut Key," he repeated. "It looks like a great place."

She lifted her brows. "You've...researched us?"

"Endlessly," he said. "I'd really like to see it."

He would? Maybe Savannah was right. He wasn't going to be a hands-off father. "You should visit us," she said, cringing as she said it because Savannah really might kill her for making the offer.

He hesitated a second. "If I didn't have a show to film, I'd be there on Thursday," he said. "Wild horses couldn't stop me. But, sadly, Netflix can."

Wild horses, huh? Did Savannah know that? Beck wanted to warmly tell him he was welcome, but that wasn't her place.

"Okay, nine o'clock on Thursday," he said. "I guess Jessie and Joshua won't be back by then."

She let out a little laugh. "My, you are familiar with the goings-on around here."

"Savannah likes to talk and I..." He chuckled. "I actually like to listen."

Apparently, he wasn't kidding. "Okay, well you want *everyone* there?" For pedicures?

"You can have twenty or more," he said. "Let Savannah invite anyone and everyone she wants."

Maybe she was wrong about the pedicures. "For...what?"

"Oh, that's a surprise. But I promise you, I know she is in a tender condition, so you have nothing to worry about. I've covered all the bases and cleared this with her doctor."

"You have? Cleared *what*?"

"Hey, I have to go, Mrs. Foster."

"It's Beck."

"Beck," he repeated. "Tell Savannah I'll check in later, but please, not a word. Not a single word. Promise?"

He sounded so sincere she had to agree. "I promise."

"Great. Let her just...enjoy the experience. I need to run. Thanks for your help."

"Sure. Bye." She tapped the phone and stared at it for a moment, puzzled and, oddly, pleased. He sounded like a nice guy. Rich, famous, handsome, and...nice. Odd combination. But a good one, especially if he was going to play a role in her grandson's life.

She headed back into the room and kept her promise and refused to tell Savannah a single word about the call. Whatever he had in mind, she was going to do exactly as the man asked and let Savannah enjoy the experience.

"What's that song you're humming, Mom?" Savannah asked a little while later, pausing in the act of dealing a game of gin with Ava.

"Am I humming?"

"I know what she's humming," Lovely said, looking up from a crossword puzzle. "It's *Wild Horses*. Rolling Stones, 1971. Quintessential Jagger holding back on the histrionics for once and wailing with real frustration about unshakeable devotion."

Ava grinned. "Lovely is like a walking 1970s Wikipedia page."

"Every folk song is a masterpiece," Lovely said. "Best on vinyl, of course, but I've lost so many over the years."

"You know you can listen on your phone now, Lovely. To any song ever made."

"Ever? Really?"

Ava smiled. "Would you like me to make you a Spotify playlist?"

"I don't know what that is, but I want it," Lovely said, beaming at Ava.

"She's right about the song," Beck said. "That's what I'm humming. *Wild Horses*."

"My favorite line in that song is so beautiful." Lovely leaned forward and closed her eyes. "'No sweeping exits or offstage lines...could make me feel bitter or treat you unkind.'"

Savannah stared at her. "Wow. Are those the words? That's so...poetic."

"Isn't it? Why are you humming it, Beck?" Lovely asked. "Secretly listening to my seventies rock records?"

"Oh, I don't know." But she did know. Because the echo of Nick Frye's words stayed in head. *Wild horses couldn't keep me away.*

Could that be true? Could he be...genuine, this actor Savannah liked to call "a professional liar?"

Wouldn't that be an unexpected twist for Savannah?

CHAPTER TWELVE
KENNY

"*Y*ou don't have to leave." Maggie leaned a little closer and nibbled Kenny's chin, dragging her hand down his chest, and sliding one long leg over his.

And every cell in his body danced to a new level of life—a level they'd been trained to ignore, sleep through, and survive with an ice-cold shower.

The fact was, he *didn't* have to leave. Ava was at Lovely's house, probably eating popcorn and watching a rom-com from the eighties.

He and Ava had finally had that talk and he let her tell him that she was petrified that dating Maggie meant forgetting Mom. He did his best to assure her that wouldn't happen, and they'd reached a shaky truce that ended with a rare hug.

He'd planned to tell all that to Maggie tonight, after a dinner with two of her friends. He was going to tell her that Ava would definitely be coming along with them to Atlanta this weekend, too. But ever since they'd gotten back to her ranch house on Little Torch Key, they hadn't done much talking.

They'd barely stayed vertical, either. They were currently sprawled out on her sofa with a pretty white cat staring at them from the back of a chair, making him a little self-conscious as they made out.

"I think it would be weird to come home to Beck's house tomorrow morning," he said, doing his best to ease them back up to a seated position just a bit. One more inch and she'd literally be on top of him, and clothes were starting to feel...optional.

Which shouldn't bother a normal red-blooded sex-starved forty-year-old man.

So why did it?

Was it just because he'd been with exactly one woman since Elise died and that had been an abject, unmitigated disaster of a sex fail? He shuddered at the thought of his attempt with a woman he'd met in the grief group that Bill had talked him into attending a few years ago.

Thank God, she'd been in as bad of shape as he was, and they both just cried their eyes out until morning. He'd never gone back to the group, and he never again saw...Denise? Danielle? Her.

That couldn't happen with Maggie.

"You're over-thinking this," she said softly, resting her head on his chest.

Because that's what he did.

"Beck couldn't care less what time you get home," she added. "And, yes, I know she's technically your mother, but it's hardly a walk of shame at your age." She splayed her fingers on his chest and looked up. "I'm an adult.

You're an adult. And we are in a new and exciting relationship that needs to..." She added some pressure. "I'm walking a fine line here, Gallagher. Somewhere between letting you know I'm ready and...begging."

He laughed softly. "You don't have to beg."

"Then..." She wrapped her arms around him and gave a gentle tug. "To the bedroom with you, big guy." She added a kiss on the lips, long and intentional. "It's time."

"Is a clock ticking?" he asked on a laugh.

"We've gone out, what? Ten times? It's time. Trust me, I like to do things the right way and this..." She nuzzled into his neck and sucked softly. "Is the right way."

It sure felt good, but...right?

He lifted her chin and kissed her mouth, doing his best to shut down his brain and heart and soul and whatever it was screaming at him that this *wasn't* right. Because she was sexy and willing and they'd been dating for more than a month, and what *wasn't* right about sleeping with Maggie Karras?

Something. Damn it. Must be Ava and all his... baggage. Or maybe he didn't want to waltz into Coquina House at nine in the morning with a just-got-laid grin.

He didn't exactly know, but something was screaming in his head. And he needed to listen. He gently broke the kiss and looked into Maggie's incredible midnight-black eyes.

"Begging," she whispered, dragging her hand lower. "Is best done on your knees. Should I..."

He threaded his fingers through hers, hating himself for being *that* guy...but being *that* guy. He wasn't nineteen. He didn't have to respond.

"You know, Maggie, when we were talking the other day?"

She searched his face and then pushed back to a slightly safer and saner distance, letting out the tiniest sigh of frustration. "About?"

"About...us."

"Oh, dear. An *us* conversation." She crinkled her nose. "I'm not a huge fan of those."

"Why not?"

"Because right this very minute, I want to drag you to bed and talk tomorrow. Don't you?"

Yes. No. He had no freaking idea what he wanted but *why* wasn't it *this*?

She sat up a little, and so did he, trying to figure out how he could share what he was feeling without losing her completely?

"I think," he said, "that considering the fact that I have a kid and...that I've been married before? I just think that I take this all a little more seriously than you do."

She stared at him for a long moment. "How seriously?"

"Do you have a problem with a committed relationship?" he asked. "I know you've said you want to have fun, but is that *all* you want? *Ever*?"

"First of all, I don't have casual sex, if that's what you're implying."

"I am not, I swear. I'm just not the kind of guy that has sex without a commitment. It's not in my DNA."

Her brows drew into a perplexed expression. "What kind of commitment?"

Oh, man. He had no idea how to answer that. "I guess...a forever one?"

She blinked at him. "Have you checked the calendar lately? The 1950s was a long time ago, dude."

"I know," he said on a laugh. "And I know how out of touch that sounds, but it's true."

"It's not *normal*. And I refuse to let you slut shame me because I want to engage in an activity that is one hundred percent healthy, safe, and wonderful. You ate dinner, didn't you?"

He inched back, unable to understand the analogy.

"Well, that's a normal bodily function. It's healthy. It's what we were made to do. It's what humans do. Eat. Sleep. And—"

"No." He placed a finger on her lips before she could utter something he would hate.

"Oh, boy." Her voice rose in frustration as she pushed all the way up. "I do not like being made to feel like some kind of...of...lowlife because I want to have sex with the man I'm dating and am not anywhere remotely ready to talk about...*forever*." She practically choked on the word.

"Maggie, please. I'm not trying to make you feel anything."

"That's for sure," she snapped back, smoothing her hair and tugging at her top like he'd tried to get it off. Which he hadn't because apparently, he wasn't *normal*. "Maybe you should go now, Kenny."

She pushed up and picked up the still-full wine glasses, carrying them into the kitchen.

"Maggie, don't." He stood and followed her, putting his hands on her shoulders to turn her around and salvage this.

She put the glasses on the counter but kept her back to him. "I don't want a serious relationship," she ground out. "I had one and it blew up in my face."

"Oh." He gave her shoulders a squeeze. "Why didn't you tell me that?"

"Because I don't talk about it. And I'm not going to talk about it now."

For some reason, that hurt. She'd sleep with him but wouldn't share her history or life? "Are you sure?"

"Positive." Then she spun around, Greek fire in her dark eyes. "But I'm not going to apologize for wanting to have sex with you."

He opened his mouth to respond, then rethought his answer, swallowing for a moment.

"I'm not going to apologize, either, because there's something in me that just can't..." He huffed out a breath. "Look, you don't want to tell me about your past? That's fine. But I do want to tell you about mine. Ava warned me that by dating you I might be forgetting my past and I promised her I would not let that happen."

An expression he couldn't quite interpret crossed her face, but she didn't say a word.

"I have had sex with exactly one woman in my entire life."

Her eyes popped. "*What?*"

"You heard me."

"Why? How? Is...something wrong with you?"

Why did she make it so physical? Didn't she understand there was so much more to it? Why did he know that and she didn't?

"There's nothing wrong with me," he said, his voice tight. "I enjoy sex as much as the next guy."

She arched one brow just enough to show she didn't believe that, which kind of ticked him off.

"I had a great..." He could never call what he and Elise had "a sex life." It would be an insult to that amazing woman. "I had a great marriage," he finished. "Healthy and normal, as you would call it. Also, deeply... meaningful which I know, I know..." He held up a hand to stave off the mocking. "Not on this year's calendar. But it's true."

Her shoulders dropped. "Wow. Lucky. For both of you."

"It wasn't luck," he said without a second's hesitation. "It was..." He swallowed, not wanting to admit the truth, even to himself. "We were in love from the time we were Ava's age."

"I remember. You met in church."

"Youth group, technically."

She crossed her arms and gave a quick laugh. "I can't compete with that."

"I'm not asking you to compete."

"You're not?" She shook her head. "I think you are. And I'm glad you had such a fabulous marriage, Kenny. You're one in a million, which I suspected, but now I know. I'm just one *of* the millions of people who don't happen to agree that sex has to move mountains and make the angels sing. It just has to feel really good, be mutually agreed upon, and safe, right?"

Wrong.

"Oh, Maggie. I hate that it's come to this," he said after a minute. "I really like you. I really hoped..."

"I like you, too," she said, looking up with eyes so

impossibly beautiful he almost changed his mind and dragged *her* to the bedroom. "What should we do?"

"I have no idea, but I do know that I'm not quite ready to—"

"I know, I know." This time she held up her hand. "You're not ready for that."

"I was going to say I'm not ready to give you up. If you heard me, I told you I haven't dated anyone in five years. You are the first person I've ever met who..." He put his hands on her shoulders and around her neck, letting them tunnel into her glorious hair. "I want to try to make this work. But I need to know there's a chance for more than just fun and sex and casual connections. I'm an all or nothing kind of guy and I want to see if this could be all."

"So no sex until you know that?"

He smiled. "No sex until *you* know that."

She melted a little, tentatively putting her arms around his waist. "You drive a hard bargain, Gallagher."

"Then I'm adding a line item to the deal."

"Oh, God, now what? You want me to go to church with you?"

"I want you to tell me what happened in that relationship to turn you off love forever."

"Kenny! You just said the L word."

"I'm serious."

"I'm getting that impression," she quipped. "Let me think about it, okay? Not tonight. Not yet."

He studied her face, memorizing the thick lashes and big eyes and delicate bones and that sweet, sweet mouth. "Soon," he whispered. "Next time."

"Maybe next time."

He lowered his head and kissed her lips, lightly but long enough to know he'd made the right decision. It had to be more than casual for him. Damn it.

THE LIGHTS WERE STILL on in Lovely's cottage when Kenny drove by on his way home around ten thirty, making him impulsively hit the brakes and turn into the shell-covered driveway. Would Lovely and Ava hate having company for one of their movie nights?

He hoped not. He missed Ava, especially this new, talkative, occasionally-gives-a-hug version who'd emerged since they'd been living in Coconut Key.

As he walked up the front stairs, he heard Lovely's three little terriers start to bark. Well, two barked. The one who imagined herself a bodyguard—Pepper, he believed—gave a threatening growl worthy of a German shepherd. A very small, stout German shepherd.

"It's me, Lovely," he called. "Come to crash the sleepover."

"Oh dear, Kenny. Brace yourself. I'm gold."

Did she say gold? Another hair dye? The purple and pink job she'd let Ava do on her gray hair back in June had just recently washed out.

She opened the door slowly, making him suck in a breath and let out a laugh at her face which was covered in a sheet of shiny gold plastic with holes for her eyes, nose, and mouth.

"We're doing twenty-four karat face masks," she explained. "It's beauty night."

He chuckled, getting a genuine kick out of the fact

that Ava had this kind of family and companionship in her life. "You look like...the Tin Man. Only in gold."

She laughed and patted the mask stuck to her face. "We have an extra, if you care to join us."

"I'll pass." He stepped inside. "Is Ava here?"

"She'll be back in a jiffy. She ran a mask down to Savannah." She beckoned him into the living room, and one of the dogs instantly growled looking up at him, about fifteen pounds of brown fluff.

"Easy, killer." He bent way down to give a friendly pet, then straightened to take a deep breath of the ocean air coming in through the wide-open sliding glass door, everything smelling faintly of popcorn and salt air. "No wonder Ava wants to spend so much time over here. Thanks for letting her move in for a bit, Lovely."

"Oh, please, I'm the one who should thank you. That child is a dream with a heart of gold. Real gold, not the plastic kind on my face."

He smiled at her, so wishing his mother could be here to agree. And Elise, who would have loved this colorful woman. And would have jumped on the gold masks in a heartbeat.

She gestured toward the sofa. "We're drinking lemonade, but I can spike some for you."

"Plain is fine," he said, pleased she didn't assume he was stopping by and running off. Maybe he had no place here at this girls' night in, but he wanted to stay. "What makes you say that about Ava's heart?"

Lovely headed into the kitchen. "Because she simply couldn't have fun unless she knew Savannah was, too. So she took a mask down to share with her so she didn't feel alone. Wasn't that sweet?"

"She's a good kid," he agreed.

"The whole time we're gabbing and laughing, she's texting Savannah, worried because Peyton and Beck went out to buy Savannah's birthday present and decided to have dinner in Key West."

"She's attached to Savannah." Kenny never tired of thinking of how his daughter had risked her own life to save Savannah's. As a father, he had been extremely upset at the time. But as a firefighter and paramedic, despite his current state of semi-retirement, he was proud of her fearlessness.

"She certainly is."

"I wish she'd take to Maggie like that," he mused.

Lovely came back with a glass of lemonade. "I bet you do. You seem to have taken to her." She eased into the chair across from him, looking at him with nothing but bright green eyes peering out from a golden face, which was both comical and some-how...safe. It was easy to talk to a person wearing a mask.

"I have taken to her," he admitted, the raw emotion of the night still close to the surface. "But I'm not doing a very great job of showing it."

"You're not?" She sounded surprised. "You seem to be very attentive and kind. You take her out. You only have eyes for her when she's in the room. Oh, yes," she added. "I watch things like this with interest. I have lovedar, you know."

"Lovedar?" He almost choked on the sweet concoc-tion they all called "Lovely's Lemonade."

"It's a gift," she said coolly. "And Maggie is a fasci-nating woman," she continued. "Something about that hot Mediterranean blood which I imagine..." Behind her mask, her green eyes widened.

"You imagine right," he said wryly. "Maybe too Mediterranean for me."

"How so?"

He took another sip and put his feet up on the ottoman, feeling truly relaxed for the first time all night. Why didn't he feel that way with Maggie? Why did she have him just the slightest bit on edge at dinner, like he was dating a stranger? And then, at her house, he was on edge in a completely different way.

"We kind of see relationships differently," he said. "She thinks they should follow a certain timeline and I think..." He shook his head. "Too serious."

"What is? This conversation or the way you see a relationship?"

"Both." He slugged some more lemonade, noticing that Lovely just sat and quietly waited for him to continue, as if she somehow sensed that he needed to. "Not that I'm opposed to the relationship she wants to have. I'm human, despite what she thinks."

"I'm kind of following, but maybe not," Lovely said. "She thinks you're a robot?"

"She thinks that people should..." He looked down at the lemonade then back up at the faceless woman who suddenly felt like a lifeline. "She's perfectly comfortable with casual sex," he told her. Well, he told the mask because it was easy. "Like, more than comfortable. She thinks it's normal and...healthy was the word she used."

"And you don't?" Lovely asked with the intonation of one of the many therapists he'd been roped into seeing after Elise died. None had ever really helped him, but they all asked questions the same way, without any judgment. And right now, it felt good to have someone listen and ask those questions, especially someone who was, after all, his literal blood grandmother.

"I struggle with it," he admitted. "I think it should be part of—no, no, I think it should be the *essential heart* of a relationship. And I know that's old fashioned and not very, I don't know, typical male."

"I don't think you are a typical male," Lovely said.

One of the dogs barked, jumping off the other chair and launching toward the open sliders.

He squinted into the darkness, spying Ava on the patio.

"There you are, honey," Lovely said. "Your father stopped by."

She came in, wearing the same gold mask, making him chuckle. "You look...expensive," he said.

"I know why," she whispered from behind that mask.

"Why you look expensive? Because you're twenty-four karat—"

"Why you don't want to hop in bed with her."

He sucked in a breath, a whole new raw emotion rising up. "Not cool, Ava. You had no right to eavesdrop."

"I didn't on purpose. I came quietly up the back stairs so the dogs didn't go nuts. I didn't mean to listen to your conversation."

Shame marched up his chest, hating the fact that his sixteen-year-old had heard that confession.

"Noneya." He used the word Elise had brought into their family, hoping it kept the intrusion light and changed the subject fast.

But Ava lowered herself on the sofa next to him. "Dad. I'm not a child."

"Actually, you are."

She looked skyward with a grunt. "I'm sixteen. I know all about sex. I know what two people do when they date."

"Two committed, preferably married people," he reminded her almost without thinking about it.

"Exactly." She reached up and tugged at the top of the mask. "And that's why you have issues."

He just stared at her as she peeled the layer of gold plastic from her face, slowly revealing her forehead. Then her eyes, which were shockingly sincere and clear as she looked at him.

"It's God."

He inched closer as her cheekbones and nose appeared—so much like Elise's, it nearly strangled him. "What did you say?"

She dragged the thick gold over her mouth and jaw, and finally she became Ava again. "I said it's because of God."

"I don't know what that means," he said.

She let out a breath, almost like an adult sliding down to a child's level to explain something simple. "You don't want to have casual sex because that's what you believe in your deepest heart is right because of God. Your faith. Your Christian beliefs."

"Ava, I don't—"

"Yeah, you do," she interrupted him with enough flippancy that he wanted to call her on it, but right then, he really couldn't talk. "Look, I know I was just a kid when you and Mom were...when Mom was still alive. But I wasn't blind. I stood with you guys in church after my Sunday school lessons were over. I watched how you were with each other. I know that there were three people at the head of my family."

His eyes stung but he kept them locked on his daughter, fighting the next wave of some unnamed and unfamiliar emotion about to rise up in him. "Three?" he managed to ask.

"You and Mom and God. That's what she always told me. She told me that you two made every decision with Him in mind. Am I right?"

So, so right. "That was a long time ago, A."

"But it was always that way. And I know it changed when she died, but I'm just being real, Dad. You can't change that much. You can't forget that you believed all that, too. And I talked to Grandma Janet about it, you know."

No, he didn't know. He was too busy living in a fog of grief.

"And she didn't do or say anything that wasn't straight out of the Bible." She turned to Lovely. "I told you, my Grandma J was serious about God."

Lovely nodded, silent and rapt at the conversation.

"Well, Dad, can't you see that? You might have stopped going to church or praying or doing whatever you did when Mom was alive, but the same stuff is going on in your heart. You still believe in what it says in the Bible and I know there's a commandment about sleeping with someone you're not married to."

"Adultery," he whispered. Because somewhere, deep in his gut, he *did* believe that. He was raised on it. He built a marriage on it.

And *that* was the something that stopped him tonight.

"Wow," he whispered, nearly speechless at the lesson his little girl had just taught him.

"Am I right?" she asked, flipping her hair back and suddenly looking sixteen again.

"You might be," he admitted. "It's been a long time since I thought about...that."

"Maybe you should." She reached for a black box on the ottoman. "Wanna do a mask? It's amazing." She patted her face. "Total life improvement."

He smiled. "You're a total life improvement, A." Reaching over, he took one of her hands. "How'd you get so smart?"

"Mom." She grinned. "Just kidding. It was Savannah. And Lovely. And Beck. And, yeah, Mom."

Lovely chuckled and patted her own face. "Get this thing off me, Ava. I'm slathered."

She popped up to help and Kenny stood. "I'll leave you girls to your movie."

"*Pretty Woman,*" Ava said. "Lovely said it's a classic."

"Even I've seen that one. Enjoy." He brushed her cheek with a kiss and walked out, taking the steps slowly as the conversation settled on him.

Was she right about all that? Was it really his dead, or at least dormant, *faith* keeping him from a normal, healthy sexual relationship? Was his daughter that smart that she knew what he didn't?

He was still thinking about it as he parked in front of Coquina House and took the back steps to the veranda. Up there, he turned to take one more look at the sky, marveling at an almost full moon spilling a river of silver over the ocean.

It was beautiful. It was...holy.

He closed his eyes and let out a breath. Was *that* the hole in his heart? And here he thought it was Elise he'd been missing all these years.

He eyed the moon and pointed at the sky. "Don't. Don't try to get me back. I haven't forgiven You and I'm not going to. Ever."

CHAPTER THIRTEEN
SAVANNAH

*T*hirty years old. *Thirty*. Almost eight months pregnant, single, jobless, living with her mother, on bed rest.

"Happy Freaking Birthday, Savannah Joy Foster." Savannah stared into the bathroom mirror and conjured up a pathetic smile. It could be worse, right? It could always be worse.

She applied a little bit more mascara and fluffed the hair she'd just blown dry. She couldn't say she hated the way she looked pregnant, so that much was good. The hormones had made her skin glow and her eyes bright. The weight was all in her basketball belly, which was awkward but not awful. Her hair was thick and luxurious, which was an added baby bonus.

So at least she looked good for her early morning birthday Zoom call with Nick Frye. The first time they'd see each other since that Christmas night.

Their phone conversations were frequent, once a day and sometimes more, but she'd held off a video call because somehow that just made this too...personal. Too intimate. Too real.

Plus, it actually hurt to look at him, he was so stinking cute.

But he'd twisted her arm into a birthday Zoom—and at six AM his time because he had to be on the set at seven. So that was in...ten minutes.

"Knock knock, birthday girl!" Mom's voice floated from the bedroom. "Are you up and about and ready for... your big day?"

"Nothing is big about it. Except my belly." She came out of the bathroom as her mother rounded the bed, arms outstretched.

"I'm so glad you were born, Savannah Joy."

"Thanks for carrying me." She patted Mount Baby. "It's true that you have to experience it yourself to understand what a sacrifice you made. And three times, Mom. Truly heroic." She kissed her mother's cheek then pulled back, taking in Mom's own made-up face and white sundress. "You look all pretty and excited."

"Celebrating my girl's big day. Nice to see you up and about."

"Well, the call, you know."

"Oh, I know."

Savannah eyed her mother curiously, the sing song voice kind of...off. "What does that mean?"

"Nothing, nothing at all." She moved to the window, pulling open the plantation shutters to let the blinding sun in. "It's a perfect day, too. Look how calm the water is. Like glass out there."

"Yep. A perfect day for bed rest."

Mom threw a look at her. "And a birthday."

Hearing laughter out in the house, and a man's voice, Savannah frowned. "Who's here? I thought it was a no-construction day."

"Oh, that's...you know. The usual group. Kenny and Bill and..." She started fussing with the comforter. "You want to make the bed before you get on your call? Make the room look more put together?"

"Uh, I'm getting right back in it, so, no. Why are you acting weird?"

Before she could answer, the phone dinged.

"Go." Mom said, her voice rising a little. "Get the call."

"That's just a reminder to get on Zoom."

As she walked to the bed to get the phone, for one insane minute, Savannah imagined that the man's voice she'd just heard out in the house was...Nick. That this was all a ruse and he'd come to see her on her birthday. It felt like she literally lost her balance for a second at the thought of someone doing something so incredibly...*romantic.*

Stop swooning, Sav. Yes, it was fun to imagine a man so thoughtful and sweet and kind. But the father of her baby wasn't a dream man, he was a celebrity, with a big job and an even bigger ego, and he was three thousand miles away.

"Okay," she said, tapping the link as she settled into her pillows and hoped she looked beautiful. Not that she cared what Nick thought, but still. "Then you can leave, Mom. I have to hold it together, so I'd like to not have my mother in the room."

Mom laughed. "Of course. You go right ahead. I'll come back later and hear all about it."

When she left, she didn't latch the door, which made

Savannah wonder if Mom was planning to stand out there and listen. She almost pushed up and made the effort to go over and lock the door, but her phone flashed with a live Zoom call.

"Happy Birthday, gorgeous mother of my child."

Oh.

She blinked at the screen, doing her best not to suck in a breath because, really, did the man have to be so perfect? She'd done her level best not to look up pictures of him like Ava had. She'd tried to forget that he had a face that was somehow masculine and gorgeous, and that surfer-blonde hair, and eyes the exact color of the sky behind him.

"Thanks. Looks like the sun is up early in California."

He laughed softly, taking a few steps so the camera phone sort of jostled, then he pulled the phone closer so she couldn't see anything behind him as his face—that *face*—filled the screen.

"How are you feeling today?" he asked.

"Pretty good. Kinda...old and fat, too."

"You don't look old or fat. In fact, you look amazing."

His voice changed when he said that; it was low and soft and...*right outside her door.*

Chills exploded over her entire body as a strange little whimper escaped her throat. "Nick."

"Right here, babe." He stepped into the room and lowered the phone. "Bringing your birthday surprise."

She tried to speak, tried to mouth the words "what the hell are you doing" but nothing came out. All she could do was stare at him and remember that seconds ago, she thought of this and dismissed it because who could be that thoughtful and sweet and kind and...*romantic*?

Well, evidently, Nick Frye could.

Not a muscle would move except her eyes, which followed him as he strode across the space and came to the side of the bed. There, he dropped on the edge, carefully slid her phone out of her hand, and smiled.

"Surprise," he whispered, leaning close to plant the softest kiss on her forehead.

"Wow, do you know how to make an entrance."

He looked right into her eyes. "Not mad, are you?"

She was a lot of things right then, but mad wasn't one of them. "I don't know. Should I be? Was my mother in on this? And...who else is out there?"

"Your friends, family, my crew."

"Your crew?" She sat up a little. "Like, you brought your entourage?" She choked softly. "You are such a celebrity."

"No, my crew. My actual, physical crew. For the yacht."

"The...excuse me?"

"The yacht. She's called *The Legend*, and she's moored about a mile right out there. Actually, you can see her out your window."

The yacht? *The Legend?* "What are you talking about?"

"Ships are referred to as women, Savannah," he said as if that was what she asked. His gaze dropped to her belly. "Can I?" he asked, lifting his hand.

"Can you...touch me? How do you think we got into this predicament in the first place?"

He let out a sigh that sounded like he'd been holding it for months then spread his fingers and laid his hand lightly on the highest part of her stomach. "Wow," he whispered.

She didn't respond, but studied his face, his eyes shuttered as he gazed down and stared. "Will he move like you told me he does?"

She put her hand over his, trying to ignore the electric shock of the skin-to-skin contact and slid his palm a little to the left, then gave the tiniest push. Almost instantly, a wee little foot kicked right back.

Nick gasped, his eyes popped, and a laugh that could only be described as pure joy bubbled up. "That was him!"

"It sure was. Saying hello."

He added some pressure of his own and got another kick. "Oh, hello, little buddy. It's me, your dad."

Savannah bit her lip and tried to swallow. He wasn't going to just disappear or throw money at her on this kid's birthday or be any kind of an absentee father. Nick Frye was all in, whether Savannah liked it or not. He wasn't going to let this baby live and not know his father, which was...

Oh, God. She didn't know what it was, except not simple. Nothing about this was simple. "I'm so confused," she admitted.

"Don't be. I took a private jet here and landed in Key West late last night, where the yacht I rented for the day was located. This morning, we motored right up here to Coconut Key to get you and everyone Beck invited for a day on board *The Legend*. We've got a whole spa staff ready to do massages, facials, pedicures—I understand you're in the market for one. And you said you were planning a yacht for the day."

"I was...joking." She managed a laugh, shaking her head.

"We're going to sail all around the Keys, with music and food. I hired the best chef I could find and he's actually—"

"I can't go on a boat!" The realization and bone-deep disappointment hit her harder than that baby could kick.

"Yes, you can."

"I'm on bed rest. And a boat is how I got bed-resty in the first place."

"No, that was in a hotel room in Santa Monica," he teased with a wink. "I've cleared this with your doctor."

"My doctor? You talked to her?"

"You mentioned her name and I called myself. She's very sweet and said you have a check-up tomorrow and she hoped that I could stay long enough to go with you."

How was this possible? How was this even happening? "Are you?"

"If you still like me tomorrow."

"I'm not sure I like you today."

He cracked up. "Then wait until I tell you how we're getting you out of here."

"How?"

"Like Cleopatra on her bed, with no less than four strapping dudes ready to do the work. They will not drop you."

"You can't be serious."

"You said it was your birthday dream, which I am here to make come true."

Her jaw just slipped a little looser.

"And then, we have a special vessel to take you to the yacht that will be driven over completely calm water very slowly. Not a single bump in the process. I promise."

"Nick, I can't—"

"You can and you will. And everyone's coming along for the very best day of your life. It's a Turning Thirty Party the way it's done in Hollywood." He rubbed her belly, somehow having gotten completely comfortable with his hand on her. "We're going to have a blast and by the time this day is over, you know what's going to happen, don't you?"

She'd be lost, hopelessly in love, and all other men would be ruined for the rest of her life? All Savannah could do was shake her head.

"We'll name this boyo! That's the goal. By the time I get back on the jet and head to L.A. tonight, we'll have a name picked."

"But what about a plan?" she whispered, the words catching in her throat.

"I think a day on *The Legend* is a great plan."

"No, for...the future. For his life, and mine? Where will he live and who will have custody and how will this work?"

He smiled, revealing those straight white teeth and some legendary dimples. "Let's start with a name, Savannah. It's just one day."

CLEOPATRA INDEED.

Nick Frye, professional actor—didn't that make him a professional liar?—hadn't lied about that mode of transportation, which was ridiculous and hilarious and an experience Savannah would never forget. How could she? Ava had danced alongside the "litter" as they called the platform with a lounge chair that they carried her on, taking pictures to memorialize this testament to the phrase *Be careful what you joke about.*

No one would listen to Savannah's protests that she *could* walk, that she was perfectly capable of strolling to a car and driving to wherever they were going, but no. She had to be carried like a queen because it was her birthday.

Nor had he lied about the "smooth ride" in a pontoon out to the yacht. Not one bump, not one wave, as if his powers included calming the waters, too. And he sure hadn't colored the truth about a yacht.

The Legend was seventy-five feet of mind-blowing luxury with a crew of five, three levels, expansive decks with leather sun beds and outdoor bars, four elegantly appointed cabins, and a living room that looked like it had been ripped from the pages of *Architectural Digest.*

And now, after her dramatic and Instagram-worthy entrance, Savannah was settled on a wide double outdoor bed-chaise-thing enjoying the traveling spa that Nick had arranged just for the party.

The yacht was so big that she barely felt the movement over the water, gliding along with the Keys to one side and the wide-open water to the other.

She sipped a Pellegrino in a crystal champagne flute under a massive sun umbrella, her feet dipped in bubbling water as a sweet lady prepared the hot stones and cucumber slices that apparently were all part of a proper pedicure.

On the lounge next to her, her mother and Lovely

were getting manicures, while Peyton lay face down all oiled and rubbed by a professional massage therapist. They were all drinking mimosas, Mom's favorite, and Savannah suspected the champagne in their glasses was the hundred-dollar-a-bottle kind.

Kenny and Bill were on a different level, fishing, while Ava just bounced around the place, exploring, then returning with animated details of every room on the yacht, sharing pictures she'd taken along the way. Maggie hadn't been able to make it, due to a meeting with a new client, and that seemed to suit Ava just fine. And Kenny, too, though Savannah wasn't sure how she knew that.

Nick floated like a true host, but mostly sitting next to Savannah on the wide bed charming them all, making sure the crew had attended to their every need. He wore a navy polo shirt and khaki shorts, the outfit looking perfectly yacht-like and showing off the impressive physique that Savannah remembered all too well.

"Having a happy birthday?" he asked on a whisper so that only she could hear.

"This is *insane*, Nick. You are insane."

"You don't even know me."

She sighed and lifted her flute in a toast. "To your admirable and remarkable efforts to change that."

"This is no effort, Savannah," he said, lying back next to her with his hands locked behind his head. "This is the fruits of my labor and a few phone calls. Getting to know you? Now that's an effort."

"I've taken and returned every call," she said. "I haven't made it difficult."

"You blocked my number the day after we, uh...met."

She slid him a look, narrowing her eyes. "Did you even try to call?"

"Twenty times."

Snorting, she shifted on the bed. "You're lying."

"Okay, ten. Five, but I thought about it twenty times... a day."

"Forgive me if I have a hard time believing that."

He shrugged and turned on his side, propping his head up to stare at her. "You always call me a liar. Why is that?"

"Oh, I don't know. Maybe because you didn't tell me who you were the night we met. You failed to mention the wife you had."

"We were separated. It was Christmas night, and I was alone getting coffee. How many times do I have to tell you that is not the life of a married man? It was the life of a lonely man who isn't as happy as people think he is."

Could that possibly be the truth?

"The divorce is final, by the way. If you want me to send copies of the paperwork, I will."

Her heart skipped the next beat, which kind of infuriated her. She didn't really care about his divorce, except how it would affect the baby.

"Congratulations," she said, lifting her mineral water again.

"It leaves me free to live my life however I like."

"You were kind of doing that before the divorce was final, weren't you?" She sipped and closed her eyes.

"You guys! You guys!" Ava darted onto the massive deck. "You are not going to believe who is on this boat!"

"I think it's a ship, grasshopper." Savannah shaded her eyes and smiled at her niece. "And at the rate things are going, you could say just about anyone and I wouldn't be surprised."

"Tag Jadrien!"

"What?" Peyton popped right out of the face hole on her massage table. "Are you serious?"

"He's the best chef I could scare up in the Keys," Nick said, as if apologizing. "The reason I could get this charter on such short notice was that their usual chef was on vacation, so my assistant did some digging and we got Jadrien." He looked from one woman to the next, clearly not interpreting their shocked expressions. "Is it a problem?"

"It's not a problem," Peyton assured him, gathering up the towel over her bathing suit as she got up. "But I need to talk to him."

"Finish your massage, Peyote," Savannah said, pointing at the table. "I'm pretty sure our captain here can get the chef to come to the deck and we can all talk to him."

She shook her head. "No, no. I need to talk to him privately first."

Savannah's brows raised. "Dude, if you are negotiating for a job with him if Jessie sells her restaurant, I will lose every ounce of respect I ever had for you."

Peyton threw her a disgusted look as she passed. "What kind of traitor do I look like?"

"Can I come?" Ava asked.

"No."

Ava's jaw dropped. "Fine. I'll go fishing with my dad."

When they both disappeared, Nick turned, looking confused. "There seems to be some drama that you've failed to share. Is Jessie selling her restaurant?"

Why did he care? How did he even remember these details she chatted about on their late-night calls? Why was he so darn perfect? Oh, the questions.

Mom, finished with her manicure, came over and filled him in on the whole situation, talking to Nick Frye like he was just another normal guy Savannah had brought home to the family to meet. Except she hadn't brought him anywhere and he wasn't normal.

Even though he acted that way.

"Do you think she should sell?" he asked Savannah, his expression genuine as if he took an active interest in the small family-owned restaurants of Coconut Key. Now, that was good acting.

"We all think she should fight him to the death," Savannah said. "And that's probably what Peyton headed down to tell him. You don't think he'll poison our lunch, though, do you?"

Nick laughed, the sound a sexy rumble from his impressive chest. He always laughed like she was the funniest human he knew. More payoff from the acting classes.

"I'm happy to taste everything first to make sure you don't all keel over dead," he said. "By the way, I told him no raw fish for you. And, of course no alcohol in the recipes. And I know that eggs make you kind of queasy, so I told him to leave those out of anything."

She dropped back on the warm leather, still not quite able to believe...well, anything. "Are you for real?" she asked on a whisper. "I mean, seriously. Are you really that nice?"

"Yeah," he said, laughing with Beck at the question. "Ask your mother. Do you think I'm legit, Beck? Or do you think I'm a Hollywood dirtbag who doesn't care about the well-being of his unborn child or the woman who is carrying it?"

Mom studied him hard, but it was Lovely who stepped closer, holding her just-painted fuchsia fingers straight up. "I'm the best judge of character I know," she said.

He grinned at her. "I have no doubt of that, Lovely. What's your verdict on me?"

"I think you're sexy, charming, loaded, and fascinating."

He snorted a laugh. "Okay."

"I also think you really do care about Savannah's welfare and you most certainly are going to be part of our lives whether we like it or not." She tipped her head and added a smile. "I personally like it very much."

"Let me get you a refill, Lovely. We can toast to that." He jumped up and walked to the bar, leaving Savannah to look at her mother and grandmother, who were looking right back with nothing but perplexed expressions.

"You two are such sell-outs!" she said on a whisper. "Give the women some Dom and a free mani on a floating tub and you're ready to name the kid Nick."

"Come on, Sav," Mom said. "He's awesome. You made us think he was some kind of slick player mired in deceit and trickery."

"Like chartering a yacht for my birthday isn't trickery." She pointed a finger at one, then the other. "Don't let me fall for it, you two. Don't let me get swept up in all this...lifestyle."

"Sorry, but there are worse ways to go," Lovely said.

She looked at her mom, practically pleading for common sense.

"Savannah, he certainly seems genuine."

"He's an actor, Mom. He fools people for a living. I don't trust him. I can't." Just then the baby kicked, hard. She rubbed the spot as Nick turned from the bar and came closer. "Neither does…"

"Sebastian," he said. "I really, really like Sebastian."

"Oh, interesting," Lovely said, taking her freshly poured champagne and OJ. "Would we call him Bash?"

"Over my dead body," Savannah said, fighting a smile as Ava bounded back in.

"Are we naming the baby?" she asked, folding in half at the bottom of Savannah's lounging bed like that was home to her now. "I still really like Ashton."

"My vote's for Corbin," Beck said. "If I ever had a boy, I wanted to name him Corbin."

"I had a crush on a guy named Sinclair," Lovely said. "Isn't that a great name?"

"Are we doing crushes?" Ava asked. "Then Levi. Or, oh, Quinn. And Ryan."

"How many crushes have you had?" Savannah asked on a laugh.

"You could just go with something classic," Lovely said. "Like John or Mark or—"

"Bill." Bill cruised in with Kenny right behind him, proudly displaying a fish. "Bill's a great name."

"Is his last name going to be Frye?" Kenny asked.

"I hope so," Nick answered.

"Really?" Ava's eyes grew wide as she looked at Savannah, who had no idea how to answer that. Who decided? "Then how about French?"

"French Frye!" They all shouted, howling with laughter.

And so it went, picking baby names from Aaron to Zachary, cracking up with Nick, and having exactly what he said she'd have...the best possible birthday in Savannah Foster's life.

Oh, heck, it might be the best day in her life.

As she looked up at Nick and found his gaze on her, French Frye kicked while Savannah's heart started to melt ever so slightly.

CHAPTER FOURTEEN
PEYTON

*T*he galley, no surprise, was like a dream kitchen. When Peyton stepped inside, she almost forgot why she'd left the comfort of the deck. She just wanted to...touch everything. And then use it to make one of Jessie's magnificent recipes.

But then the man at the prep station made her remember why she'd come down here—to warn Chef Tag Jadrien not to tell anyone she'd asked him to write the cookbook Introduction. The very idea had kept her up at night and even had her walking by Coconut Tropics a few times looking for his Tesla, but she'd never spotted it there. Had she, Peyton might have dropped in to ask that he bag the whole thing.

Since they'd talked, she'd done nothing but second-guess her impulsive decision, which was one of the reasons Peyton Foster spent most of her life waiting for something to happen. Because when she made something happen, she drowned in doubt.

"Peyton?" He adjusted his rimless glasses, his eyes widened in shock. "What are you doing here?"

"I'm a guest of Nick Frye's," she said, not minding that the role gave her a tiny bit of confidence to face down the famous chef. "It's my sister's birthday."

"Your sister is Savannah?" His brows lifted. "Oh, yes, I knew this. I met her that night at the restaurant in Key West. But I didn't know she was *this* Savannah." He gestured toward a magnificent cake with spun sugar and over-the-top decorations and thirty candles, of course.

"One and the same. I heard you were our chef today."

He lifted a shoulder. "When a celebrity calls..."

"You answer," she finished.

He tipped his head toward the stainless counter with a somewhat sheepish look. "I'm doing crab cakes...with lime. I hope they're as good as yours."

She had to laugh at that. "Pretty sure you'll knock the crab cake out of the park."

"Unless you want to do the same ones I tasted. Do you have the recipe memorized?"

"I do, but..."

"Cook with me, Peyton." He snagged an apron hanging on a hook and held it out. "I'm told our host is quite the carnivore, so I'm doing a tenderloin for the lunch entrée. I call my rub 'fire and spice.' Would you like to learn it?"

More than anything. But she also had to talk to him, so maybe this was the opportunity to do both.

"Sure," she said, taking the apron and tying it on. "I'm surprised you don't have a *sous chef* on this fancy ship."

"I don't really need one for a group this small.

Anyway." He threw her a smile. "Any word from Jessie? How's the family doing?"

"I guess it's pretty rough," she said. "Jessie's sister owns a small coffee shop-diner place and needs some help, so they're staying a bit longer."

"Foodies in the family," he mused. "I'm glad she's able to help."

She eyed him, wondering about this man who seemed to care about Jessie.

"So tell me, how does your sister hobnob with such famous folk?" he asked.

She knew that Savannah wasn't keeping the "relation-ship" a secret and she could tell from what Nick said that he wasn't either, so she jumped right in. "She's pregnant with his baby."

His expression flickered with surprise. "Oh. I see."

He probably didn't. No one really did, but she let it go and reached for the bowl. "Is this your crab mix?"

"Yes. Please taste and tell me what it needs."

She grabbed a clean spoon and took a tiny bite the way she'd seen Jessie do a hundred times. "Scallions," she said without much hesitation.

"Good call. There's some in the fridge." He jutted his chin toward a massive Sub-Zero that took up half a wall. "The place is well-stocked, I will say that."

"It's a dream," she agreed, getting the scallions and rinsing them in a vegetable sink.

"So, about that, uh, favor I asked you."

"It's done. I was going to bring it by tomorrow."

She froze in the act of pulling a knife from the block. "Done? You wrote it already?"

"It's only two pages," he said on a laugh. "I blog a lot

and that kind of prose comes easily to me. Also, it came from my heart. It was quite simple to write, considering I know nothing about the cookbook."

She immediately felt a little better, the first bit of doubt waning. "Oh, I'm glad. I wasn't sure how you'd approach it."

"You do realize I've known Jessica Cross, er, Donovan, nearly my whole life?"

"I know that you two knew each other when you were kids and lived on Coconut Key." She also knew Tag "lost" her to panty-melting Chuck Donovan and that his real name was Taggert Lutwack, a boy as awkward as his name.

"I stood next to her the very day she chopped her first onion."

"In Home Economics?" She couldn't help smiling as she revealed that she knew this fun fact. "She did tell us that."

"She did?" He sounded hopeful. Was Taggert Lutwack still harboring feelings for Jessie Cross? Then why put her out of business? "It was the best learning experience of my life," he said, quite serious. "We both discovered a love of cooking we didn't have any idea we had. Neither of us were raised in particularly 'cooking forward' homes. But for that half a year, she and I were like kids at an amusement park. Each ride was more fun than the one before."

"Was that what you wrote about in your essay?"

"For one page, yes."

She diced the scallions, a little nervous that her knife skills were lacking under the watchful eye of this renowned chef. But he didn't seem to notice. "And the second page?" she asked.

"I wrote about you."

"Me?" The knife froze mid-chop. "I'm the editor. I shouldn't have anything to do with this book."

"I didn't mention you by name, but think about the function of an introduction in a cookbook, Peyton. What are you trying to get the reader to do?"

She slowly started to chop again. "To understand what to expect on the pages. Maybe get some perspective on the author." The truth was, the piece in most non-fiction was a marketing tool, and a way to elevate the author's credibility. Which was exactly why she'd so impulsively asked the only celebrity chef she'd had handy to write one.

"I think you're getting the reader to buy," he said, showing that he did understand why she'd asked him. "I think of a person flipping the book open in the bookstore or touching that 'look inside' button online and what's the first thing they read? The Introduction."

"That's true." She gave him a look as sheepish as the one he'd given her when he copped to the crab cakes. "You do have a big name." She added a smile. "And I even know the real one."

His eyes flashed with something close to horror. "You do?"

"Jessie told us."

She could have sworn some color drained from his face. "I need to tell her not to do that anymore."

"Why?"

For a moment he just stared at the spice rub, as if

thinking very hard about something. He swallowed, took a breath, and turned to her.

"About the cookbook Introduction," he said, in a voice that felt like he was more of a professional actor than the guy up on the deck above them. "I talked about you because you told me you were, in essence, a rookie. And not only could you cook Jessica's recipes, they nurtured that same love for cooking that I discovered at her side in high school. You know what it made me think?"

She shook her head, pausing in the chopping to look at him and listen.

"That is Jessica's magic," he said softly, making her notice he'd slipped into her formal name that hardly anyone used. "Not just her recipes, but her...style. Her presence, if you will, which I am going to assume is on every page of the book. She helped nurture a love of cooking in me, too. She's a nurturer...of people, of flavor, of passions."

It was so true. A natural nurturer who should have been surrounded by kids and grandkids. "You're right," she said, dumping the scallions in the mix. "I hope that works for her."

"Oh, it won't," he said on a laugh. "She'll whine and say, 'I'm not riding his coattails' because that's what she does every time I approach her."

She considered that as she started forming the patties, her attention split between the crab mix in her hands and the way he skillfully seasoned a tenderloin.

"Can I ask you a favor, Chef?" she said after she made a few patties.

"Of course."

"I haven't told Jessie yet that I asked you to do this. So

do you mind not mentioning it when you come upstairs to the party? I mean, I assume Nick will want everyone to meet you."

"Will they hate me?"

She smiled. "They are on Team Jessie, not going to lie."

"Then they should like me even more," he said. "Because, Peyton, I am the current captain of Team Jessie."

"But you want to put her out of business."

"I want to save her from losing everything. Again." He added that last word on a soft whisper that made her turn and search his face.

"You really are doing this to help her?"

"Why is that so hard to believe? Yes, I really want to help her, and I have my reasons for that."

Because he still had a crush on the pretty girl in his home economics class? Or was it something else?

It was hard to believe he cared that much about Jessie, but if someone had told her Nick Frye would be the father of her sister's baby and take the whole family on a yacht, she wouldn't have believed that either.

"Can you tell me this much?" She finished the last patty and started transferring them to a baking sheet. "Is Jessie going to flip out when I tell her what I've done?"

"Cooked with me? Maybe."

"Enlisted your help on the book."

He blew out a breath and smiled. "She might. But that would be foolish and you and I both know that. It won't help her cause to delete my pages."

"Her cause"—she fixed a slightly misshapen patty —"is to keep the restaurant from going under. This is our effort to save her from...the competition. You know that, don't you?" The minute she said it, she felt better. Honesty was always best.

But he just laughed and slapped the tenderloin noisily. "Of course I know that. Why do you think I'm helping?"

"I honestly don't know."

He looked her right in the eyes. "I only want the best for her. If the cookbook brings her enough business to stay afloat, then I'm all for it. If it doesn't, she has a backup plan and won't lose everything." He turned and looked right into her eyes. "Now, how are you with a nice mango chutney?"

"I've made it once. It's in the cookbook."

"Would you make it twice, or would you rather get back to the party?"

Truth? She was happiest right here in the galley. "One mango chutney, then I'll go back." She smiled up at him. "Thanks, Chef."

"No, Peyton. Thank you. You have no idea what a gift you've given me."

No, she didn't. But sometime, when she got back, Jessie was going to have to come clean.

CHAPTER FIFTEEN
SAVANNAH

*S*avannah was as close to sleeping and still being awake as a person could be, suspended between the real world and her dreams, her body gently rocking, the sounds of an old Van Morrison song floating from hidden speakers. Through it all, a large, warm, masculine finger stroked her knuckles.

Wait a second.

Savannah's eyes opened but before she could snatch her hand away, Nick clutched it tighter. She turned to see him lying next to her on the tilted leather lounge bed, the massive deck empty, but the soft voices of her family and friends laughing somewhere on the deck above them.

"You awake now?" he asked gently.

"I wasn't really asleep."

"Beg to differ."

She winced. "Snoring?"

"Not at all," he assured her. "Just peaceful and relaxed."

"Oh, that I am. What an incredible day."

"Look, Sav." He lifted their joined hands to point to the right side of the yacht. "The captain brought us around to the Gulf side. Check out that sunset."

She tore her gaze from his face—no mean feat for a mortal woman—and looked to the right, drinking in an orange and peach and purple sky that quite literally took her breath away. The water was a mirror image of the colors and clouds, glasslike and still, shockingly beautiful.

"The Keys sunsets are something, aren't they?"

"I've never seen anything like that," he agreed.

"Even in California?"

He grunted softly, his eyes fluttering closed as if he didn't even want to think about California. "If I had to run away from home like you did, I'd come here, too."

"L.A. wasn't my home," she said. "I was only there for a year. Portland before that, which I hated. And a stint in Colorado, where I learned photography. Many addresses." She gave his hand a squeeze. "I'm what you call a...leaver. No moss, no roots, no nothing under my feet."

"You're about to have a kid. I heard they're always underfoot."

What exactly was he saying? "So my tumbleweed ways are coming to an end." She purposely made it a statement, not a question. Because there really wasn't any question. "I can't drag the Child With No Name all over creation looking for..."

"What *have* you been looking for?" he asked when she didn't finish.

"Ooh, deep."

"Well, there must be a reason you move so frequently

and don't want roots or moss to grow under you. What is it?"

"I don't know. Others have asked, and I only say that I get itchy. I want to move on to the next adventure. The next good thing. I'm that person at a party who's always wondering if there's someone else I should be talking to than the person in front of me, then I get home and I realize I never had a substantive conversation with anyone."

"And how does that make you feel?"

She laughed. "Like I should call them all and apologize."

"I'm the opposite," he said. "When I go to a party, I find one person I want to talk to and they're wearing me for the night."

"I bet the lucky lady doesn't mind at all."

He groaned. "You seriously don't know me, Savannah. You are making things up based on garbage in the media and one experience you had with me."

"Maybe, but having been that lucky lady one night, I know the power of being the center of your attention." Like right now, with those gas-flame blue eyes burning right into her soul. "It's intoxicating."

"Are you intoxicated, Savannah?" He didn't make a single move closer to her, but somehow she felt a magnetic draw and, yeah, it was dizzying.

"High on sparkling water and life and..." She turned away. At that point, it was a matter of survival. "That gorgeous sunset."

Another song started up, this time the high-pitched siren call of Joni Mitchell.

"Someone's stuck in the seventies," Nick said on a laugh.

"That's the playlist that Ava made for Lovely," she said. "And no doubt Ava figured out how to hook it up to the sound system like the true teenager she is. And, yes, my grandmother is stuck in the seventies."

"That's when she had Beck?"

She smiled. "It always amazes me that you listen."

"Why?" he asked. "Why are you so determined to think the worst of me?"

She studied his face again, lingering over his lips, remembering exactly what they felt like that one night he'd used them so effectively on her. "Oh, I don't know. Maybe because you're gorgeous, rich, famous, and I don't trust your motivation."

He sat up on a soft choking laugh. "That's so not fair. I flew here, chartered this yacht, and can't take my eyes off you. What don't you trust?"

"Why?" She turned a little, which woke up Junior, making her automatically put a hand on her belly to rub him back to sleep.

"Why did I do all this? For you. For your birthday. To show you that I...care."

"Why do you care? Just because I'm carrying your baby? There are so many ways to handle that issue—all of which are currently on the table but none of which include this over-the-top attention. Why are you doing this?"

He dropped onto his back, letting her hand go so he could lock his fingers over his chest. He looked like a dead man, staring up at the sky...or someone who just fell onto the shrink's couch.

Also, he had a perfect profile but that was no surprise.

"I was raised by a single mother," he said softly. "My father disappeared when I was a baby. He never showed up again, until after I got famous, then all of a sudden, he wanted to be my best pal. My mostly-drunk cliché of a loser-living-in-a-trailer kind of best pal."

She swallowed, imagining what a betrayal that must have been, but not wanting to interrupt.

"And my mother did her best as a single parent, but she's never going to win the Mother of the Year award, either. Stage mother, maybe, but for all the wrong reasons. She made me realize that"—he turned to her, his eyes tapering as he made his point—"no one should be on their own when raising a kid. It's a two-person job for a reason."

"Is that why you're here? Doing all this? For..." She patted her belly. "French Frye?"

He snorted a soft laugh. "Forever his name."

"Only if his last name is Frye."

Nodding, he let that go. "To answer your question of why I'm here, yes. He got me here, but I did want to see you again, Savannah. I liked you from the second I met you. I never forgot you."

"You meet a million women, all of them perfect, and I imagine every one of them is ready to be at your beck and call."

"But I *like* you. I don't meet a million women I like. And maybe they are perfect on the outside, but they're not funny or real or smart. And you *ghosted* me. Blocked my number, social media blackout. Why?"

"You were married."

"Separated," he insisted on a sigh that sounded like

he was sick of reminding her of that. "Anyway, most importantly, I am responsible for...French Frye." He put his hand over hers and gave another little rub. "I can't shirk that responsibility. I can't walk away from you, or give you money and a wish for good luck, or see the kid once or twice a year and call that being a father."

She sighed, emotions rolling around just like the baby's foot against her abdomen. "That's obviously beyond admirable."

"I disagree. I think it's baseline stuff. But that's just me."

"And I can't say no even if I wanted to, because I'm sure you'll be a great dad and a total asset to this child's life."

This time he waited, looking expectantly.

"But so will my mother and grandmother and sisters and friends," she said. "I have to say that seeing L.A. in the rearview mirror of my car the day I left to come here was one of the best sights of my life. I don't like living there, but I suppose..."

"I'll take care of you financially," he said.

"Oof." She turned and closed her eyes. "Dependent. I hate that word almost as much as I hate bed rest."

"It doesn't make you dependent, it makes me responsible."

"I know," she nodded. "And I'm grateful. As far as dumb one-night stands go, I chose wisely."

"It wasn't dumb."

"It wasn't smart," she countered.

"We used protection."

"Apparently you need some more effective armor, dude."

"Maybe this baby was meant to happen, Savannah."

She groaned and rolled her eyes. "Thanks for the cruel joke, universe."

"I'm serious," he said, reaching for her. "Maybe this little guy is going to cure cancer or change the world or start a civilization on Mars or write the greatest love songs or paint that sunset right there."

She had to smile. How could you not in the face of such passion and optimism? "He really is lucky to have you as a father."

"And you as a mother," he volleyed back. "I've seen you with Ava. You're a natural, you know."

"Someone else got her to sixteen. It's the little years that scare me. When they can't talk or do anything but poop and cry. That's why I need this village of amazing women, Nick. I can't handle that without..." She gave a self-deprecating laugh. "Without my mother. How sad is that?"

"It's kind of beautiful, if you ask me. And so...is this song." He slid her a look. "You're able to get up, right?"

"For emergencies."

"This is a dance emergency. Now playing is my number one all-time favorite song."

"You want to dance?" She smiled at him, listening to the strains of a new song, another from Lovely's seventies playlist, a few heart-wrenching guitar chords filling the air.

"What is it?"

"*Wild Horses* by the Rolling Stones."

"Really? My mother was just humming that the other day and Lovely recited the lyrics."

"Dance with me..." He got to his feet in a graceful

move, holding out his hand and singing a few words in tune with Mick Jagger. "I'll sing the lyrics...in your ear."

She laughed softly. "You'll never get close to my ear with a beach ball between us."

"Let me try."

How could she not? She took his hand and did her best to match his grace—and probably failed—then let him guide her to the middle of the deck, where he slid one arm around her waist and took her hand in his.

She looked up, remembering how small she felt, even at five-six, with a man who was easily over six feet. They looked down at the bump between them, chuckling a little, but somehow, miraculously, they fit. Mostly.

The baby pressed against him and he managed to splay his hand on her back and just hold her in a way she couldn't ever remember being held. Like she was precious and valuable. She couldn't quite comfortably lay her head on his shoulder, but she was able to look right up at him as he looked down at her...and sang.

"'Wild, wild horses...couldn't drag me away.'"

Her heart fluttered as he whispered the words to the song she and her mother had just been talking about, each word coming out slow and deliriously seductive and evocative. Lyrics about aching pain and sweeping exits, sins and lies, and broken faith. Right then, it felt like the songwriter had looked at this crazy situation with Nick Frye and Savannah Foster and picked up a pen to write poetry about it.

The golden orange glow of a magical sunset reflected in his eyes, his gaze locked on her. Savannah swayed in his arms and just felt her whole being falling... falling...*falling*.

This cannot be happening. It can't.

But as the song came to a sad, sweet ending about someday...Nick lowered his face and gave her a kiss that matched the poignancy of the moment.

And Savannah knew that no matter what happened, where she lived, how this child was raised, or by whom... she'd always be grateful to little French Frye for giving her the single most romantic moment of her life.

CHAPTER SIXTEEN
BECK

*T*he day after Savannah's birthday, the sense of serenity that was somehow magically created onboard *The Legend* was still palpable in the air. Beck and Ava and Lovely sat at the kitchen table sharing pictures and reliving the experience while Peyton whipped up a batch of scones.

"You know what's next?" Beck asked on a whisper. "The baby shower!"

"Oh, yes," Lovely agreed. "We need to get her all the things she needs."

"She needs Nick," Ava said, making all of them turn to her, surprised. "I mean just look at those two dancing." She tilted her phone toward Beck.

"Wait, what? How did I miss that?" Beck squinted at the phone, then gave up and grabbed a pair of reading glasses to see better. "Holy...wow. Was this when we were all on the upper deck listening to music? After dinner? I thought Savannah was napping."

Lovely took the phone and peered at the image, taken from above, but it sure looked like they were about to kiss. "Yep. My lovedar was screaming last night."

"Lovedar?" Ava and Peyton both snorted with laughter, repeating the word.

"I can smell love," Lovely said with a shrug. "It's my superpower."

"Get out." Ava laughed, then came closer to Lovely. "Like, for real? Do you smell pheromones or something?"

"I know people," she replied. "I can read them. That boy—I suppose I should say that man—is smitten."

"Am I the subject of breakfast chatter?" Savannah's voice floated in from the living room as she came into the kitchen, making a rare appearance. "I smell scones," she added at their surprised look. "And I have a doctor's appointment in an hour. Mr. Smitten is taking me."

Lovely clucked and looked a little too smug, which got a glare from Savannah.

"Did I hear you right?" Savannah asked. "You have lovedar?"

"Oh, I do, but it doesn't make me a psychic," Lovely told them. "I'm one of those people who get a sense when something is genuine and when it isn't. I can read non-verbals and I'm old enough to see things you all can't."

"What about Dad and Maggie?" Ava asked.

"Whoa. Wait. Me first." Savannah eased into the chair across from Lovely. "What did you see yesterday with Nick?"

Lovely turned the phone she was still holding to show the picture to Savannah. "You tell us."

She studied it for a second, her expression softening

imperceptibly before she flicked her wrist. "Oh, that. We thought it would be fun to balance French Frye between us."

"French Frye." Ava cracked up.

"So you are going to give the baby Nick's last name?" Beck asked.

Savannah let out a sigh that made her whole body melt a little. "You guys," she moaned. "The man is confusing me. He really does seem to...care. Is that possible?"

"Of course!"

"Why wouldn't he?"

"Just look at you!"

She waved off the avalanche of assurance and beamed at Peyton, who brought her a tea and scone. "Thank you, sweet sister." She wrapped her fingers around the cup and looked from one to the other. "I appreciate the support and enthusiasm, but you *do* realize that any kind of relationship with him, whether it's platonic co-parenting or...whatever Lovely's lovedar is reading, means I'd have to live in California." She curled a lip and picked up the scone. "Mama no like California."

"You can't leave," Ava said, the agony in her voice a perfect reflection of the feeling in Beck's heart. She'd waited thirty years to truly understand this complex and layered daughter of hers, and now...she'd leave?

"And take my grandson?" The question slipped out from Beck's lips before she could stop it.

Savannah gave a sad smile. "It's complicated, Mom."

"How do you feel?" Lovely asked, putting a hand on Savannah's arm. "What do you want?"

"I don't know," she said honestly. "I can't see beyond October second, when what's-his-name makes his grand entrance."

"Levi," Ava said.

"Corbin," Beck added.

"Sinclair." Lovely tapped the table. "Anything but *French*."

"Why can't I pick a name for this kid?" she whined, breaking the scone.

"Because that makes him real?" Beck suggested.

"He was pretty real while he practiced soccer at four this morning," Savannah said, taking a bite. "Maybe this'll settle him. Oh my God, Pey-o-tay!" She grinned around the bite, using the old nickname for her sister. "Don't tell Jessie you just beat her in the Great Scone Race."

"Really?" Peyton turned from the stovetop where she was filling a basket with more. "You think they're that good?"

"Almost as good as the two meals you let Tag Jadrien take credit for yesterday," Beck added, smiling at her oldest daughter. "I recognized Jessie's recipes and your deft hand."

"Seriously?" Peyton came back to the table with the basket of scones. "I actually changed the recipe a little. I think these should be your signature scone for Coquina House."

As they all helped themselves to the scones and groaned with appreciation, Beck tried to get the conversation back to Savannah. She was hurting and scared, and the group of loving hearts around this table could only help her.

"Wasn't the goal of yesterday to finalize a name?" she asked Savannah. "Did you do that or come close?"

She shook her head and took a sip of tea. "He really likes Sebastian, which...isn't that a character in a Disney movie?"

"He's a crab in *The Little Mermaid*," Ava informed them. "I think you can take that one off the list. What's wrong with Levi?"

"You know what's wrong?" Savannah asked, looking from one to the other. "We don't know his last name. Does it have to be Frye if we're not really a family? What's the protocol of the name?"

"I think it can be whatever you want," Beck said. "You could hyphenate it."

"Foster-Frye?" Savannah snorted. "I love him too much to saddle him with that. But I do need to know what that name will be."

"Maybe you guys will talk about it more today after the doctor's appointment," Peyton said.

"Maybe, but he has to haul back to L.A. and be on the set this afternoon." Savannah reached for Ava's phone. "Can I see that picture again?"

"Sure."

They all nibbled on scones while Savannah stared at the phone. "We danced to *Wild Horses*," she told Lovely. "He was crazy about your playlist."

"That's not on her playlist," Ava said. "Trust me, I know. The last one from Lovely's list that played was that high pitched whiny lady asking for help."

Lovely sliced her with a look. "That was Joni Mitchell. Show some respect, child."

Everyone laughed, except Savannah who was still

trying to wrap her head around this news. "So, who played it?"

"The steward," Lovely said. "He said it was the host's request."

"Nick? So we could dance to it?" Savannah looked stricken by the idea.

"What's wrong with that?" Beck asked.

She just closed her eyes. "He's making me believe him, that's what's wrong. He's making me trust him. He's making me...want him."

"Oh, what's that buzzing I hear?" Lovely cocked her head and put a hand behind her ear. "Must be my lovedar."

Savannah stood, picked up her tea, and looked at Beck with that same expression she'd wear as a little girl when she was confused about homework or had a problem with a girlfriend.

"I need to get dressed," she said, stepping away. "Lovely, shut that lovedar down."

"Never."

"Grasshopper, forward me that picture, will you?"

"Of course."

"Pey-pey, keep cooking. You're better at it than anything you've ever attempted before."

"There's a compliment buried in there somewhere," Peyton said with a wry smile.

"And, Mom?"

"Yes, honey?"

She jutted her chin toward the veranda. "Bill's outside waiting for your date."

"It's not a date!" she exclaimed. "We're doing B&B research."

"Tell that to Lovely's lovedar." Finally smiling, she left the kitchen.

Beck leaned around Lovely to see the veranda, where Bill was on the phone, his back to all of them.

"It's *not* a date," she insisted under her breath. "Why would she even say something like that? He's just very flirtatious. I imagine he's like that with all women, right, Ava? You know him. He's just a super-friendly guy."

All three of them just stared at her.

"Oh, please." She rolled her eyes and pushed up.

"Sorry," Ava said. "But I think you make a sweet couple."

"But..."

Just then, the slider opened and Bill walked in. "Ready to roll, gorgeous?" he asked. "I got us a walk-through at that Haven place so we can scope out ideas, and I just pulled up a list of boutique hotels, inns, and B&Bs throughout the Lower Keys."

"I already made one," Beck said.

"Great, we'll have two, but I made some appointments to check out their best rooms."

Wow, he was very serious about this analysis, and Beck appreciated that. "Did you tell them we're building a competitive place?"

"Oh, no. I told them we were getting married and looking for a place to spend our honeymoon."

He did *what?*

Or *not* so serious about it.

She just gave him a tight smile. Peyton turned back to the sink so Beck couldn't see her reaction. Ava looked a little smug. And Lovely was doing that thing with her ear again.

Oh, boy. Could be a long day.

AFTER THEIR TOUR of The Haven, Beck knew exactly why the stunning property was on the market for an eye-popping price.

For one thing, this side of the island was different from the Atlantic side, with fewer palm trees on the water and a much more traditional sandy beach. And definitely where the very most expensive houses were located.

The three-story beach house with a small guest house sat steps from the sand, accessible by several driftwood-colored ramps and steps. The house itself was an eye-catching mix of Victorian mansion washed in a coastal vibe, painted a dreamy shade of pale blue with wrap-around porches trimmed with white railings.

The best part, at least in Beck's opinion, was a second-story turret-style balcony that was perfectly situated off the main living area to enjoy drinks, watch some breath-taking sunsets, and then relax as the moon rose over the water. And a huge wooden deck with a summer kitchen and seating for big crowds and parties.

Inside, the calm coastal color scheme and elegant, but comfortable, furnishings appealed to a woman who'd spent a whole lot of the last two decades decorating a large home. Every one of the five bedrooms had been professionally decorated, and the massive living areas felt like they were part of the most high-end accommodations.

Light poured in from more windows than she could

count, bathing the all-white chef's kitchen in warm sunshine. Even the guest house, which was a complete two-bedroom apartment with its own kitchen and garage, was exquisitely appointed.

If she could recreate even a smidgeon of all that? Coquina House would be a dream. As she and Bill walked back to her truck, she shared her thoughts and how much she loved the place.

"I told you there's a market for high-end in Coconut Key," he said, opening the door and giving her a hand up to the passenger seat.

"Is there? That house has been on the market for two months, probably because of the price tag."

"It's fully furnished." He closed the door and came around the truck while Beck gazed up at the back of the beachfront mansion.

For a moment, she almost felt like the real couple Bill wanted to pretend to be. She'd talked him out of it for this walk-through, but sitting here, talking purchase price and house décor felt very natural to a woman who'd been married for thirty-four years.

And as he got into the car and smiled that slow, devilish grin, she felt a few other things that were probably natural, too. But not quite...right.

He started the truck and leaned down, squinting through the sun at The Haven. "That sure is a beauty," he said. "I'd love to build a house like that."

"I loved every inch of it," she agreed. "But we need to see B&Bs today. Where to next?"

"The Mar Brisas Inn on Sugarloaf Key."

"Oh, I've seen that online," she said as she pulled her

seatbelt on. "I think it's very similar in size and scope to Coquina House, unlike this beauty." She gave a wistful wave to The Haven. "That property is the stuff that fantasies are made of."

A few minutes later, they crossed over to Sugarloaf Key and used the GPS to find the Mar Brisas Inn.

"Here we are," he said as he parked his truck in a lot on the outskirts of the small town in Upper Sugarloaf. "I think this is going to be a little lower-end."

"I think it's going to be perfect."

Bill met her on the passenger side of the truck, both of them gazing up at a cheery yellow and white two-story house located on the corner of two wide canals, surrounded by lush foliage.

"Let's not do the honeymoon bit," he said as they walked to the front door.

Thank God. "Just tell them the truth? We're doing some B&B research because we're renovating one?"

"Are you kidding? And risk being kicked out?" He put his arm around her. "Follow my lead, Mrs. Dobson."

"What?"

"Just follow my lead," he repeated, pulling her into his side and leaning his head toward hers. "It'll be fun."

That was the problem. Everything with him was fun. She knew she should slip away and try to make this somewhat of a professional outing, but...she didn't.

Was that because she was enjoying this a little too much? The feel of him, the easy laughter, the way this man made her feel so young and vibrant again? Why didn't she feel that way with Josh?

Because their relationship was entirely different. It

was founded on friendship, not flirting. Respect, not romance. And it was...not quite as thrilling.

Was that wrong? She tamped down the tendril of guilt that threatened to wind around her chest and just walked with him into the tiny front room that had a desk set up to greet and accommodate guests of the inn.

"Hello." A woman about Beck's age looked up from a computer screen. "Welcome to the Mar Brisas Inn. How can I help you?"

"I'm Bill Dobson and this is my wife, Beck."

Wait. Hadn't he just said they *weren't* doing the honeymoon thing?

"Hello, Bill and Beck. I'm Angela Howard, the owner and proprietor." She came around from the desk to shake their hands warmly. "Where are you from?"

"The Atlanta area," Bill said smoothly. Okay, it wasn't a lie, but...

"Are you looking for a room? Because it being August and the season, we've got plenty of space." She added a wry smile. "And I mean hurricane season, not snowbird season."

"There haven't been any named storms," Bill said. "I thought it was supposed to be a good year for hurricanes."

"Well, there've been two, but they didn't come close to us," she said. "But now there's one called Candy who doesn't look so sweet and another one, Dylan."

"Dylan?" Beck inched back. "I didn't know there was another named storm."

Angela rolled her eyes. "He's a doozy and moving fast," she said. "And I do not like the spaghetti models. Oh, but then you probably don't watch the storm tracking in Atlanta the way we do down here in Florida, so you might not know what I'm talking about. What brings you to the Keys?"

"We're down here to celebrate our fortieth anniversary."

At Bill's statement, the woman's jaw dropped, and Beck had to work hard not to do the same. Not just because they did not need this level of details to research the place but, whoa, he was a smooth liar.

"Oh, I don't believe it!" the woman said, making Beck suddenly wonder if he wasn't that smooth after all. "There is not a chance either one of you have been married for forty years, unless you were both children. You're so young."

"We were then, too," he said. "Sixteen and..." He threw a playful look at Beck who could only stand there, slightly horrified. "Well, we have a son who recently turned forty."

That was true. They'd even had a little party at Coquina House not so long ago. But other than that, she was standing here silent, complicit in his charade.

But Angela pressed her hands together over her chest, crooning. "And you made it *all* these years after a teenage romance. What a wonderful love story. I'm sure that couldn't have been easy when you were just children yourselves."

Bill tugged Beck so closed to him she was practically up his armpit. "This woman right here? A saint. An absolute saint. I can't even imagine life without her."

"Aww." She beamed at Beck. "You know how lucky you are? Take it from someone whose marriage did not go so well. Divorced after twenty-nine not-so-happy years, dumped for a sweet young thing. But now I have Mar Brisas and I'm happy."

"You made a whole new life for yourself," Beck said, far more interested in that story than the fiction Bill was spinning. "Good for you."

"It's been a challenge, but I'm so proud of my inn. Can I show you around?"

"Any chance you have a honeymoon suite?" he asked. "We want to see your absolute top-of-the-line offering."

"All of our rooms are very similar in size and scope," she said. "They all have water views and private en suites, king-sized beds, and gorgeous antiques. Come on, I'll show you my favorite, the Calico Clam. We have five rooms, all named after seashells. We also have Rusty Dove, Junonia, the Venus Clam, and Lion's Paw Scallop."

As she chattered, Beck tried to drink in the décor, which was understated and warm, with touches of contemporary color. It didn't scream money, it whispered comfort, and she loved that.

"You've done a beautiful job with this inn," she said. "Elegant and warm."

"Thank you! I've enjoyed every moment since I opened a few years ago."

Beck could only pray she'd be as happy as Angela a few years into her Keys adventure.

As they climbed the stairs, Beck noted the beautiful wainscoting on the walls and the pretty shell artwork hanging above it. Everything was exactly how she wanted to style Coquina House.

"Here we are. The Calico Clam." She opened the door to a darling bedroom with a four-poster, a dark armoire, and a giant window that looked out over the deep blue canals, a sailboat on a dock beneath them. "There's no balcony here, but the bathroom is truly luxurious. If you prefer some outside access, let me to take you to Junonia. They're both available tonight. How long are you planning to stay?"

"Oh no, we're just looking for later," Beck said quickly, half afraid that Bill would impulsively book the inn here that very night.

"Well, then, why don't you go up to the third floor and let yourself in? Junonia's on the right, and Rusty Dove is on the left. The doors are open now. See what you think, and I'll be downstairs at the desk to set up your reservation."

With a smile, she left them alone, and Beck turned to give him a look. "Forty years of marriage?" she asked on a hushed whisper.

"Hey, a man can dream." He looked into her eyes with a gaze as dark and intense as she remembered from the nights in the Camaro. "It could have happened, Beck."

"Doubtful." She angled her head. "We barely knew each other. We were hardly high school sweethearts. You were the bad boy rocker and I was—"

"Perfection. You still are."

She smiled, shaking her head, torn between wanting to take him seriously and wanting to run screaming out of the room. When his phone vibrated and he looked at the screen as if he really resented the interruption, she chose the latter, only she didn't run and didn't scream.

While he took the call, she went upstairs and let herself into Junonia, immediately charmed by this third-floor room. It wasn't huge, but the chunky furniture fit beautifully, with a creamy white comforter and soft pink pillows that made her think of the inside of a seashell.

The hardwood floor gleamed, softened by a faded area rug. The room had a long dresser with a darling porcelain water pitcher, plus a bottle of sherry and two glasses. Nice touch, she thought, turning slowly to take mental notes.

One small room, with a balcony and a private bath. Perfect, cozy, inviting, and not the least bit...grand.

She stepped into the hall to see the other room, thinking that the layout was exactly what she could do with the third floor of Coquina House. That is, if her GC would just let go of his own far more expensive idea. Hopefully, today changed his mind.

As she put her hand on the doorknob of the Rusty Dove room, Bill's voice floated up, the narrow stairwell between them amplifying it a bit more than she imagined he knew.

"You know I'm doing everything humanly possible, man." The words sounded like they were coming through grit teeth, tense and angry. Was this a Coquina House issue? Hesitating, she waited to hear just one sentence more to see if this problem had anything to do with her construction job.

"You can't do that, Granger."

She waited a few seconds, knowing she shouldn't eavesdrop but riveted by the tension in his voice.

"I know how much I owe!" The words bounced off the walls.

He was in debt? "For God's sake, give me some time. I just need to close one deal. I'll have enough to get him off my case for a while when I get the draw. I know, I know.

I'm robbing Peter to pay Paul. Whack-a-mole. I know all your stupid analogies. Come on. I'm working on a big reno with a good profit. Gimme two more weeks and I'll have access to cash."

She pushed the door open and stepped inside, heat pressing on her cheeks. Was he pushing her to do that suite because of the profit? Because he needed money? Was that why he was flirting with her? To butter her up to save his own behind?

"Small and unimpressive."

She turned at his words, seeing him in the doorway of the room, willing her heart to stop thumping over the uncomfortable words she'd just overheard.

"This room, and that one," he said when she didn't answer. "Nothing like we're going to build, Beck."

"It's exactly like what I want to build, Bill," she said coolly. "And, you know, I've seen enough to know that."

He looked a little crestfallen. "You're not going to do the suite?"

"Why does it matter so much to you?" she asked, trying, and probably failing, to keep the note of accusation out of her voice.

"Because I want your place to be amazing, Beck. Because it's going to make you stand out in a sea of ordinary. Because you can make more money."

"Or *you* can."

He stared at her, silent, expressionless, for four, five, six heartbeats. Then he blew out a breath.

"You're the client, Beck. Let's call it a day and go home to see if those permits came in. And we can file the last one for two rooms on the third floor."

He turned and headed down the stairs, leaving her to

wonder if that victory was worth it. And why could he flirt with her but not confide in her?

In the truck on the way home, they listened to the news—which wasn't just a way to avoid conversation.

Hurricane Dylan was building speed and strength, and currently on a course directly toward the coast of Florida.

CHAPTER SEVENTEEN
KENNY

"*H*oly cow, Beck. How many windows *are* there in this house?" Kenny stood in the storage unit and stared at sheets and sheets of plywood.

Beck glanced at her mother who was plucking her way through the storage shed hidden in the mangroves at the back end of the Coquina House property.

"Seventeen," Lovely said, coming up on his other side. "And you should be incredibly grateful that we have these boards. You don't want to go to Home Depot today. The one in Key West will be a zoo and the one in Marathon will be out of every stick of plywood and sandbags."

He nodded, grabbing one of the boards to pull it toward him. "There's more than seventeen here."

"We have enough to cover the windows in Coquina House and in my cottage. And Jessie's restaurant."

He nodded, considering that...and hating the amount of work involved in hanging these boards. Just after the permits came in, too, and he and Bill were ready to deal with the subs.

But everything had taken a back seat to the threat of a hurricane, even though it was still five or six days away and could change course. Right now, it was on track for landfall somewhere between Key West and Daytona Beach, so they'd all spend much of the coming days watching that red circle move.

"And I guess the cottage and the restaurant are even more vulnerable because they face due east," he said, thinking about the track. "This house is a little protected by the mangroves and the fact that it's concrete block on the first two floors."

"Pffft." Lovely waved a hand. "Nothing is vulnerable."

Of course she said that, because from the moment they started tracking Dylan, Lovely had seemed remarkably unconcerned for a woman who had a vested interest in three waterfront properties.

"It'll turn," she said. "They almost always do."

"'Almost always' doesn't exactly give me mountains of confidence." He moved some of the boards, gauging their weight. "This could be a big one. Cat four and one of those spaghetti line things has it on a dead-on track to the Keys. That could wipe this place off the map."

She rolled her eyes. "Yeah, yeah, yeah. I've lived here seventy-three years, Kenny. We've never been wiped off any maps. There was nothing of note between 1922 and Irma, a few years back."

"Really?" Actually, he'd done some research on this. "That broken bridge off Big Pine Key? Destroyed in a hurricane in 1935."

"The old Bahia Honda bridge? Restored and used until 1980 when they built a new one. The break in it was man-made for boats, but it does serve to scare off lily-livered tourists during the hurricane season. Plus, it's a landmark now. So, yes, we've been hit hard a few times, lost power for a few months—"

"Months?" he choked.

"I think it's too early to go hammering these things everywhere," Lovely said. "But I don't have to do the work, so start when you need to. I'm going to check on the provisions in the safe room, but I'm worried it's a little small for all of us."

"All of us?" he said. "Why would we all be in the room that's built to protect valuables and heirlooms?"

"And people. During storms."

"No," he said. "No one is staying in this house when that storm comes. Or yours. Or the restaurant."

Lovely blinked at him like he couldn't be serious, but there was nothing that drove a first-responder crazier than hardcore stay-homes in a life-threatening situation.

"We'll go to your house," Lovely said. "You're more than six miles from the beach, right?"

He conceded with a nod, knowing exactly how far inland they'd have to go to be out of the evac zone. "And my place is concrete block, so yes. But you can't stay here."

"We'll watch the track." She turned to Beck, looking for support. "You lived here long enough to know this is a bunch of hooey half the time and barely a blip in our lives the other half. It's a storm, people, not Armageddon."

With that, she walked out, leaving Kenny staring with

disbelief at Beck. "She's not staying here," he repeated, pulling out his phone to tap the storm tracking app. "You do agree with that, right?"

"Yes, and if you can't accommodate us, I'll get a hotel up near Orlando."

"Let's just see where it goes." He skimmed the phone screen. "Still saying landfall in the US in five days, so Saturday night, Sunday morning. This is going to wreck our schedule because not a sub is available right now, and if it does hit? Even minor damage could throw us off. And guess what? Wherever it makes landfall? All the trades will go there for work, leaving us empty-handed. That's happened on jobs to Bill before."

"Mmmm." She turned and looked at the plywood, suddenly preoccupied with it.

"Mmmm?" He laughed softly. "What exactly does that mean?"

"Ask my daughters. They call it the Beck Foster non-answer she gives her kids when she doesn't want to say what she's thinking."

He lifted a brow. "You counting me as one of your kids now?"

"You are."

He tipped his head in thanks. "So...what are you thinking that you're not telling me?"

She let out a slow breath and glanced at the shed door as if someone might hear her. "It's about Bill."

Oh, God. She liked him. Kenny felt his whole chest tighten at the thought. Bill's flirting was working. Beck liked him. Okay, was that the worst thing in the world? They were two of his—

"I think he's in financial trouble," she said softly.

Oh. Wasn't expecting that. "You do?"

"When we were looking at B&Bs, I overheard him on a really tense call about a debt. Talking to a guy named Granger. And you know, it made me wonder if he would push me to—"

"Granger? Shoot." He snapped his fingers. "I never gave him that message. I was so wrapped up in other stuff." He shook his head, then the rest of her words hit him. "Push you to what, Beck?"

"Bite off more renovation than I can chew," she said. "I don't understand why it's so important to him that I spend significantly more on the B&B and end up losing a room, which means income, in the process."

Or why he'd left Atlanta and all his business behind to focus on one project five hundred miles away.

"I think he wants you to be really happy with the finished product," Kenny said, years of loyalty to Bill bringing a defense to his first position. "He seems to... care about you."

"You know, I thought he did, too, for whatever reason. But now I'm wondering if all that attention isn't just part of an act." She looked up with a plea in her green eyes. "You know him better than I do. Could he be doing something...not good? Could he be in over his head in finances?"

"He's never been reckless with money," he said, and this time it was more honesty than defensiveness. "He can get some big draws, too. That means a sum of money that the contractor gets to pay the subs and vendors, usually coming from a bank holding a mortgage. And GCs need to do some juggling. It's not completely out of the question, although not exactly ethical, to pay one with money from a different job to keep things going smoothly, then make it up when the next draw comes in."

"Like the expression to rob Peter to pay Paul?" she asked.

"I think that's what it means, yeah."

"And whack-a-mole?" she asked.

"Um...smacking down one problem only to have another one come up. Why are you asking me this?"

"Because that's what I heard him say on the phone," she explained. "And he was upset with this Granger guy. Like maybe he was being...threatened?" She whispered the word, but suddenly some things did make sense. And Kenny did not like the sense they made.

"I'll talk to him," he said. "I do think he's been acting a little out of character these days. I never really saw him hit on a woman like he has with you, although God knows the man is charming."

"He is," she said with a smile. "And I love his work and ideas. But something's not right."

He'd known that for a while and was mad at himself for not pushing Bill harder. Turning back to the plywood, he asked, "When do you want me to start putting it up? It'll take two days."

"If you start now, you'll have plenty of time to take it down when the storm turns."

"You, too, Beck? What's with all the non-believers around here? If this storm makes landfall in the Lower Keys, you can kiss a Christmas opening goodbye."

She made a face, clearly not loving that possible change. "I have a feeling you're going to be the one doing the lion's share of the work here, at Lovely's, and the restaurant. And it's hot as blazes, Kenny. Start now, do it in stages, and know that there's really no way I can ever thank you."

"Are you kidding? For all you've done for Ava? I can never repay you."

"You know I love that girl," she said. "And how are things with Maggie and Ava? Ava told me Maggie backed out of your trip to Atlanta this past weekend."

"Yeah, she had another new client who needed to see her on Saturday."

"That's what happened for the yacht day."

He nodded. "She's really busy." Or avoiding him. She'd come over when he and Ava moved into the house but hadn't stayed long, promising to come back soon and help with the décor.

"And did you two have that heart-to-heart?"

"Who? Me and Ava, or me and Maggie?"

She looked a little surprised. "Didn't know you needed to have a talk with Maggie. How are things going, if I may be so mom-like and bold to stick my nose in again?"

That made him smile. "I'm getting used to the mom-ness," he said. "I don't hate it."

"Anymore," she added.

"I never hated it," he admitted. "I just love my mother, the other one. The one who raised me."

"You don't have to qualify it, Kenny. Janet Gallagher was and always will be your mother, with a lot more investment and sacrifice and love than I could ever dream of matching. Just the fact that you acknowledge me as your birth mother is a tremendous source of joy for me, you should know that."

"And for me," he added, feeling a little strange being this honest, but he truly respected this woman and wanted her to know that. "And, to answer your question, I'm not exactly sure how things are going with Maggie."

"Oh." She angled her head with understanding and sympathy. "It takes time to get a good relationship moving in the right direction."

"She doesn't want to take any time." He gave a dry laugh. "She just wants to move. Fast."

"Really? Well, that's...good, I guess. I mean, if she's that serious and knows your situation as a single dad and wants to take on that added—"

"Baggage," he interjected.

"I was going to say responsibility."

"I don't think she necessarily wants to move in the, you know, maternal direction."

"Are you sure?" Beck asked.

Nothing about what she wanted to do was *maternal*. "Yeah. And even if she was..." He looked down at Beck, his thoughts about Maggie finally seeming to take a distinct shape. "I'm not sure she'd be the one I'd want stepping into that role." Maggie's beliefs didn't align with...Elise's. And didn't he owe Elise that much when he went picking a woman who'd be around Ava?

"Well, it's very soon and she's a wonderful, talented woman," Beck added.

"She is," he agreed. "But she's...I don't know how to describe it."

He didn't want to say anything that would reflect

badly on Maggie. She was who she was, guided by her own morals, and he didn't want to put that in a negative light. These were his issues, not hers.

"Whoever is in my life is a role model for Ava," he finally said. "And I have to remember that."

Beck's eyes seemed to fill as she stared at him.

"What? Did I upset you?" he asked. "Because that's not an indictment of Maggie."

"I know." Her voice was a little thick as she reached out to hug him. "I'm just so impressed by you."

"Good genes," he said on a laugh, patting her back.

"No, that's not genes." She drew back and looked up at him. "That's what Janet and Jim Gallagher brought to the table. A strong, intelligent, good man with an amazing foundation. I'm just so grateful that they were the ones who got you." She smiled. "Whoever Pastor Eugene was? The man who brought us together? I owe him a debt of gratitude."

Pastor Eugene was the man who dunked Kenny in the water, baptizing him when he was fourteen years old. Pastor Eugene was one of the ones who laid that foundation Beck was talking about.

"He's gone now," he said. "Long gone. But he was a great man."

"Hello, Kenny?" Maggie's voice broke into the hot little hut making them both turn, probably looking guilty since they'd been talking about her. "I was hoping to find you."

She stepped into the shade of the shed, looking fresh and beautiful, without any makeup and her hair in a ponytail. For a moment, he just wanted to reach out and pull her closer. The attraction was strong and real, and he wasn't at all positive he wanted to let it go.

"I'll let you two talk," Beck said. "I need to find my mother and figure out if she's serious about riding out this storm."

"She's a Conch," Maggie said. "A Keys lifetimer," she added for Kenny's benefit. "Those people never want to leave for a storm."

Beck said a quick goodbye, leaving Kenny and Maggie alone in the shed.

"If you've come looking for plywood, I might be able to spare some." He gestured toward the wood leaning against the wall. "Although I've been informed I have three buildings to board up."

"No, I have hurricane shutters on my house and I saw them on your rental, too. So you'll be safe there, but it'll be noisy. And if you don't want to stay there, I guarantee you the Gulf side of Coconut Key will be fine. My mother, however?"

"She's in Pompano Beach, right? North of Miami?"

"Yep, and she's directly on the water. I want to go help her board up, too—"

"Do you need me to come with you?"

"You're sweet," she said. "She's got a handyman doing the heavy lifting. But I'm not coming back until after the storm. I snagged my mom and me a reservation at a hotel inland if it doesn't turn."

"Good to have a plan," he said.

She looked up at him with uncertainty in her dark eyes. "Do you have a plan, Kenny Gallagher?"

"My house is safe and far enough inland," he said.

"The biggest challenge will probably be getting Lovely to leave."

"That's not what I meant," she said softly. "I meant a plan...for life."

A trickle of sweat meandered down his neck, and not only because the shed was hot and airless. "Kind of heavy for...now, isn't that?"

"I need to know," she said. "I've been thinking about this a lot, the whole time you and Ava were up in Atlanta over the weekend, and..." She exhaled with a little moan, as if that thinking had not been fun. "I'm not seeing it."

"You're not seeing...what?" Even though he already knew what she wasn't seeing.

"Kenny," she whispered. "This isn't quite what either of us want."

Looking into those ebony eyes, she sure was what he wanted. But he knew there had to be more than just physical attraction, especially when something was holding him back from acting on that attraction.

He flipped around a few arguments in his head. *We don't know what we want. We're just getting started. Give this some time...*

But they all sounded hollow.

"I guess you're right."

She got up on her tiptoes and kissed his cheek. "I hope you find what you're looking for."

"I'm really not looking for anything."

"Yes, you are. You don't know it, but you are." Her smile was tight and sad as she put a hand on his chest, tapping over his heart. "This thing in here? It's a good one, but it has a hole in it."

"Grief," he admitted gruffly.

"I actually don't think that's what it is. You're empty. I hope you find someone to fill that hole. I really do."

With one more smile, she stepped back and blew him a kiss.

He stood in the shed for a long time, more sweat stinging his eyes. At least he hoped that was sweat.

CHAPTER EIGHTEEN
PEYTON

*T*he whole idea of protecting the restaurant during a storm was a little paralyzing to Peyton, so she was grateful that Jessie had found a chance to FaceTime and "walk" around the place together. That would help Peyton prepare for the storm.

"Beck texted me that Kenny is going to do the plywood over the big windows," Jessie said. "And that's really the main worry. You just have to be sure to get everything out of the safe and take pictures. The insurance company, if we need them, has to have pictures."

"Okay, I'll get pictures of everything, I promise." Peyton perched on the edge of a chair in the dining room, looking out over a patio that never looked calmer. "It's hard to believe there's a storm out there. It looks like another sunny day in paradise."

"I'm hoping it turns and heads up the coast," Jessie said on a sigh that sounded wearier than Peyton's. "Because I'm not quite ready to come back."

"Tell me more about Heather," Peyton said. "Are you living with her? Are the kids handling it okay?"

Jessie closed her eyes like it was too much to answer. "Heather is strong and doing better than I would have expected. We've had a lot of late nights together, and I'm just glad I've been able to give her my perspective on being a widow. The kids?" She sighed. "Maddie's pretty quiet, which is really out of character, and Marc is just mad. So, so angry. Josh has been a godsend, taking Marc with him on all kinds of errands and trying to keep him occupied."

"And the café?"

"Monroe's? It's the cutest place. It's kind of a coffee shop-diner-bakery thing, right in a pretty touristy section of Charleston. But Heather does all the baking and Drew ran the business. Right now? She's lost all interest in working and is letting me handle things."

"She's in mourning," Peyton said. "She'll rally."

"She'll have to, but, whoa, it's a long road."

"I'd suggest bringing them all down here, but not with Hurricane Dylan bearing down on us. Maybe after?"

Again, Jessie shrugged. "It's a day-to-day thing up here. So, tell me good news. How's the cookbook?"

"Done," Peyton said with a victorious smile. "It's with the page formatter and I should get a mock-up to approve this week. I'll send it to you when..." She shut her mouth before she made that promise. If Jessie saw that beautiful Introduction...

"Yes?"

"Why don't you just trust me and let me give you the final product? It'll be so satisfying to hold it in your hand."

"No, I have to see it," Jessie said. "Is it too late to add something to that scone recipe? I told you it's Heather's, and she gave me the best—"

"Hello! Don't shoot me. I let myself in the back again!"

"Who's that?" Jessie asked, narrowing her eyes at the phone camera. "Did Kenny come to do the window boarding?"

Oh, God. Oh, no. Oh, *dear*. "Not sure, I better—"

"Peyton! It's Tag. I know you're here."

On the small screen in her hands, Jessie's eyes widened to great big brown circles of shock. "*Tag?* Is there? In the restaurant? Talking to you?"

"Jessie, there's something I have to tell you."

"No kidding! Peyton, what the—"

"I got him to write the Introduction for the cookbook. It's amazing, Jessie. I ended up getting to know him and cooking with him on the yacht—no one told you he was the chef Nick Frye hired—and he's really a nice guy and he only wants to help you."

The words tumbled out in record time as she tried to squeeze the entire explanation out gracelessly to beat Tag's entrance.

"It was the one time in my life I didn't want to wait for something, and I just did it and please, please, Jessie, don't be mad."

"There you are!" Tag came into the dining room at the very second she finished her plea.

"Jeez, he walks in like he owns the place already," Jessie muttered, giving Peyton some measure of relief that she didn't just hang up.

"He doesn't, and he won't," Peyton assured her, turning around to see Tag.

"Let me talk to him," Jessie said, her words tight...and surprising.

"Sure. He's right here."

Striding with the confidence he always exuded, Tag weaved through the tables and came right to Peyton, who held the phone out.

"It's Jessie. On FaceTime. She wants to talk to you."

His brows lifted as he took the phone.

"Jessie?" Peyton watched him look into the screen, adjusting his glasses a little. "I'm really sorry to hear about your brother-in-law," he said right off. "I'm sure it's a tough time."

The kindness must have taken the wind out of Jessie's sails as all Peyton could hear was her muttered, "Thank you." After a beat, she added, "I want you to stop, Tag."

The note of seriousness in her voice took Peyton back a little, making her wonder if she should give them privacy to discuss the deal.

"Did Peyton tell you the news then?" he asked. "About the Introduction?"

Scant seconds ago.

"Yes. Thank you. It will sell more cookbooks to have your name attached to the project."

"Then I'm happy to help, Jessica. As you know, I only want to—"

"If you wanted to help, you wouldn't be in Coconut Key. You wouldn't charm my employees. You wouldn't offer to buy the only dream I have left."

Tag spun around, his voice muffled so she couldn't hear the response. Sensing it really was time for privacy, Peyton got up and noisily headed out to the patio and closed the sliders to block them out.

Whatever they were discussing, it wasn't her business and she had no right to listen.

So, she started to do a mental inventory of what needed to be brought inside before the storm. All the tables and chairs. Plants, too? She should have asked Jessie. She should have asked Jessie before she overstepped her bounds with Tag Jadrien, too.

"She wants to finish up with you." He stepped outside, holding the phone to her.

She nodded thanks. "Did you need something, Chef?" she asked him, trying to make her voice sound as formal and professional as possible.

"I just wanted to be sure you had a way to board up and protect the restaurant, but Jessica says you're all set. Please let me know if you need anything at all, Peyton."

"Sure, sure."

"I'll show myself out." He gave a nod and headed through the sliders, leaving Peyton holding the phone.

"So, Jessie." She looked into the screen to talk to her friend. "I'm really sorry if I screwed up."

"You didn't," she said. "I'm surprised you let him in on our plans to crush him with a cookbook, but I think he knows...he's uncrushable."

"He truly wants to help you, doesn't he?"

"He certainly acts that way," she said.

"Maybe it's not an act," Peyton suggested. "Maybe he really does care. Maybe he feels bad he came back to Coconut Key to open a restaurant."

"Then he should close it."

"Maybe he wants another chance with you," she added on a whisper. "Is it possible he cares about you... romantically? He's single, right?"

"Divorced, but I don't know about that. It's not exactly the vibe I'm getting. But I'm grateful for the book Introduction." She gave a slow smile. "It was kind of a brilliant move, Pey."

"Really? You think so?" A shudder of pride rolled through her. "I'm so glad! I've been staying awake at night worrying about your reaction."

"You know what? It's a cliché, but it's true. Life is too precious and short to stay awake at night worrying about anything. I thought I knew that after Chuck died, but seeing my sister struggle..." She let out a sad moan. "Go hug your mother for me. And Lovely. And Savannah. And every other person you see. Love, not hate."

Peyton laughed softly at that. "I will. So, you don't hate Tag anymore?"

"I never hated him but, whoa, I'll never *love* him, that's for sure."

"But will you sell to him?"

Jessie looked at her for a long time. "Not if I don't have to. But I might be making some changes when I get back."

"Really? Like what?"

"Let me keep thinking about it. It shouldn't affect the cookbook, though. Stay the course, my friend. Thanks for being sweetest thing I ever knew."

"Thanks for being everything you are, Jessie. Everything."

Jessie smiled into the camera, and maybe teared up again. "Listen, this is your first hurricane. Take it seriously, okay? They don't happen often, but Irma kicked our butts and it took a long time to recover. Be careful. Make sure everyone is."

"I will, I promise."

After they hung up, Peyton stared out at the glass-like water, suspecting that she finally understood the phrase *the calm before the storm.*

CHAPTER NINETEEN
BECK

*P*itch black darkness permeated every corner of Coquina House despite the fact that it was nine in the morning and the September sun was already blazing on Coconut Key. But with all the windows completely boarded up, it felt like two in the morning—not two in the afternoon—as Beck walked through the house.

Lovely's little Cairn, Pepper, stayed close, following Beck's every step, clearly concerned that she could no longer look out the windows to make sure no one was approaching the house.

Beck turned on some lights to see her way to Savannah's room, where Lovely, Peyton, Ava, and the other two dogs, were holed up. All of them were huddled around the iPad currently running the Miami local news.

"I guess it's time to get our evacuation on, ladies," Beck said as she walked in.

Pepper barked as they entered, making the others laugh.

"Of course she'd agree with that," Lovely said, reaching down to pet the dog but still holding tight to the Westie in her lap. "Always on duty, this one. But, sweetie, I don't see any reason to leave yet."

"Um, the mandatory evacuation for the coastline is reason enough for me," Beck said.

"Pffft." Lovely flicked her hand. "Mandatory schmandatory."

Beck ignored that. "Fortunately, Kenny's house isn't part of the order, or we'd be driving to Orlando to find the last available hotel room. I, for one, am grateful to have a secure home on an inland street to ride out this storm."

Beck had been watching the news frequently enough to know that the northward track was actually the most common track of these storms, but right now, it looked like it would hit South Florida and they could get some incredibly strong winds, even all the way down here.

"I don't want to move from this bed," Savannah groaned, then laughed. "Probably not what you guys ever thought you'd hear from me."

"It'll be fun," Ava assured her. "We'll have a slumber party."

"Tomorrow night? There's not going to be much slumbering, grasshopper. Except for French Frye." She rubbed her belly. "He hasn't moved in hours."

Beck's eyes widened. "Is everything okay?"

"I'm fine, I promise," she assured them. "The doctor said that can happen in the last few weeks, so I shouldn't worry." She smiled. "Honestly, the only one worried about anything was Nick, who shouldn't have been allowed to ask questions of the Ob/Gyn because that ten-minute appointment turned into an hour."

"Have you heard from him today?" Beck asked.

"Twenty times. He went spiraling down an internet rabbit hole about how babies are born during storms because of the drop in barometric pressure."

Ava gasped. "Seriously?"

"Hush, it's fine. We have three more weeks in the oven."

"Gosh, I hope so." Beck brushed back her hair over damp temples as she got closer to the screen Savannah had propped on the bed. "Let me see the latest models. Landfall in Vero Beach, still?"

"If that happens, we won't even get rain," Lovely said.

"From your lips to God's ears," Peyton murmured.

Savannah reached for Beck's hand, tugging her closer, her expression darkening with concern. "You look beat, Mom. I can't stand that I haven't been able to help you."

"I'm just sweaty and I've had plenty of help. I think I've been sweating for five days," she added on a laugh.

She'd spent hours hauling boards with Kenny and filling the safe room with treasures, bringing in outdoor furniture and plants and umbrellas and anything else that could be a projectile in a category four or, oh God, *five* storm.

And the past hour, they'd packed their bags and plenty of food for the days and nights they'd be evacuated to Kenny's house. "But we're all done."

"So is my house, thanks to my darling great-grand-daughter," Lovely said, smiling at Ava. "She brought in every stick of furniture at the cottage for me."

"And the hammock?" Savannah asked.

"It's folded and safe in a closet," Ava said. "Everything is secure."

"Hey, where is everyone?" Kenny's voice preceded him as he walked into the room. "Well, here's a gathering." He greeted everyone and came closer to Ava on the bottom of the bed, holding Basil in her arms. "I knew I'd find you here, A."

"Just keeping an eye on my godson," Ava said, pointing to Savannah's belly. "Did you know babies are born in hurricanes?"

"Of course. Barometric pressure drops can bring on labor." He turned to Savannah. "You feel okay?"

"I'm fine. I just had a doctor's appointment, and everything is good; I'm only one centimeter dilated."

"What does that mean?" Ava asked.

"It means we have nothing to worry about, but since your father is a paramedic, we're in good hands."

He choked a laugh. "With rusty delivery skills, so keep it at one centimeter, Mama." He turned to Beck. "Can I talk to you for a second?" He thumbed over his shoulder to silently indicate he wanted to have that conversation in private.

"Sure." Beck followed him into the still-dim hall, through the living room, and around the dining room and kitchen, a little surprised that they needed this much privacy. "Is everything okay?"

"I don't know," he said softly, scratching a jaw that hadn't seen a razor in a few days. "Have you heard from Bill?"

"No, not since he left to help his friend down in Key West. He said he'd be back...yesterday?"

"Well, he's not back. I called his friend in Key West

and he hasn't seen Bill, and he's checked out of the hotel where he was staying."

"Well, he had to because it's closed. Could he have gone back to Atlanta? Maybe left early to beat the traffic?"

"And not tell us?" Kenny shook his head. "Something's not right."

"Did you talk to him about...what I overheard?"

He nodded, pulling out a kitchen chair and folding into it, and Beck took another.

"That was the last conversation we had," he said. "He brushed it off, said Granger's just some 'clown' who thinks Bill owes him on a project that went belly up months ago. And I know the job he's talking about, so it makes sense. The client went into bankruptcy so he didn't pay Bill, so Bill can't pay the subs."

"What happens then?" she asked.

"The GC still has to make those payments, but Bill always figures out a way to do that, and it's not a huge amount. I've called him over and over and his phone clicks right into voice mail, like he might not even have it turned on."

She could see the concern etched in his dark eyes, so very much like the eyes of the man they were discussing. "Have you tried calling his kids?"

"I exchanged voice mails with one of his daughters, the one he's closest to, who just said she hadn't heard from him for a few days but that's not that unusual. It sounded like she wasn't aware he was even out of town, but I didn't pursue it. Anyway, let me know if you hear from him, okay?"

"I think he'd call you before me," she said.

His jaw locked with tension, he looked away, silent.

"Is there more that you're not telling me?" she asked.

"Yeah, kind of. I tried calling his ex-wife, Natalie, on the off chance he'd been in touch with her. But..." He snorted. "I doubt I'll hear back from her."

"Was it that bad of a divorce?" she said, thinking of how little Bill had shared.

His eyes closed for a second, his expression hard to read in the dim kitchen. "She has a serious issue with alcohol."

"Oh." Beck leaned back on the chair. "I didn't know that."

"He doesn't like to talk about it. Honestly, he's riddled with guilt that he just couldn't stay with her, but she drove drunk with their granddaughter in the car once—"

Beck sucked in a soft breath.

"It was fine," he said quickly. "She was pulled over and arrested, which meant she wasn't allowed to be near her grandkids. That's when he finally signed the divorce papers that had been lingering for years. It broke him."

Her heart ached for Bill, for the whole family. "What a sad situation," she said. And far worse than what Dan did to her.

"I also exchanged texts with his son, but they don't really get along, so I didn't go into details about Bill's disappearance."

"Disappearance?" She gave a shiver at the word. "Would you call it *that*?"

"Three days without a word or a returned message? It's getting there."

She reached for his hand, wanting so much to give him comfort or hope. "He probably lost his phone or it ran out of battery. Maybe he's helping people he knows get ready for the storm because he knows we have you."

He gave a tight smile as if to say he appreciated the effort, but wasn't really buying it.

"You watch, Kenny. He's going to blow in here any minute, tell me I'm gorgeous, and beg me to spend more money."

He didn't laugh. "None of that is in character. Not the way he flirts with you, not the pushing for a bigger investment, and not this. He's here when he doesn't need to be, and he's acting strange. Dodgy, even. I really think something's going on in his life."

"Well, if you think he's...disappeared, then shouldn't we call the police?"

"Not yet. I have a few more feelers out. Let's just get through this storm and hope you're right."

"Well, while we're talking about him, I have a confession to make."

He gave a wry smile. "Who'd you tell?"

"Josh," she answered on a laugh. "I had to."

"It's fine. We'll figure it all out after this storm passes."

THERE WAS STILL no word from Bill the whole next day while they settled in to ride out the storm at Kenny's house. Beck found herself checking her phone more frequently, and not just for storm updates.

They were about twelve hours from "landfall" which looked like it could be close enough to make for a hellacious night, but not exactly a direct hit on the Lower Keys. With all of them glued to the television in Kenny's family room, it felt like the whole world had come to a standstill, riveted on every gust of wind that would determine how hard they got hit, if at all.

Meteorologists reported from beaches up and down Florida, a little too gleeful over every drop of rain and the dark, dark swirling clouds that Beck imagined were over Coconut Key at that moment, too.

With the shutters blocking out the world, they couldn't see much, but Kenny had left one small panel of glass uncovered on the front door, so they could have that tiny window to the outside.

Pushing up from the sofa, Beck headed to that window to watch the palm trees blowing, and heavy gray clouds building overhead when Ava came up next to her, grabbed her hand, and gave her a horrified look.

"What's wrong?"

"I left my flat iron on."

Beck blinked at her. "Where is it?"

"In Savannah's bathroom." She pushed closer to Beck. "I'm scared it's going to start a fire."

"Could it?"

"I don't know." Her eyes filled. "But I'm so scared of fire."

For the first time in a long, long time, Ava's eyes took on a look that Beck knew meant she could have an anxiety attack. They'd stopped but something like that never really went away, and with all the stress and uncertainty of this storm, she didn't doubt that panic was brewing in Ava's heart.

"Are you sure you left it on?"

She nodded. "I know I did. And Beck, please, please don't tell my dad. He'll be furious with me."

She doubted that, but Kenny had been in the kitchen making calls and sending texts, and she knew he was as stressed about Bill as Ava was about her flat iron.

"I can go check right now," she said. "I can run in and unplug it. No one will even miss me."

"Are you sure?"

"Of course." She put a hand on Ava's cheek. "Relax. Breathe. Drink tea. Rub Savannah's belly."

"She's asleep." Ava pointed to the "throne," as Savannah called the recliner they'd given to her for the duration. "Are you sure, Beck?"

"I'll be back in fifteen minutes." She fluttered Ava's stick-straight locks. "Who flat irons her hair before a storm anyway?"

Ava rolled her eyes. "Teenage girls." In that moment, she was so much like Savannah, Beck had to smile.

A minute later, Beck slipped out unnoticed, grateful her car wasn't blocked by any of the others.

The first few fat drops of rain from one of the many far-reaching bands of Hurricane Dylan smacked on her windshield as she started to drive. The back roads were deserted and even US1 was light on traffic.

Most people were hunkered down, ready for a storm...or not. They'd left town or they'd boarded up and were gathered around the TV just like Beck's family.

She drove down Coquina Court toward the house, which looked strange with all the windows boarded up and blurry from the rain that had picked up to a steady downpour. It wasn't until she got close to the house that she noticed the back end of a white truck parked so deep between mangroves on the side of the road that she barely noticed it.

Bill's truck! He was here?

She threw her car into park and instantly reached for her phone...which she'd left at Kenny's house in her hurry to get over here and put Ava out of her misery. So she couldn't call Kenny to tell him Bill was back, but... why didn't he go to Kenny's house? Why come here?

She climbed out of the car and headed toward the truck, inhaling sharply when she saw him sitting inside, his head in his hands, his shoulders moving. Was he laughing...or sobbing?

With the rain streaking the window and hitting her face, she couldn't tell.

"Bill?" she called, but he didn't hear her. "Hey, Bill!" She approached the driver's side and tentatively tapped with her knuckles, making him whip around to look at her.

His face was red, streaked with tears, but his eyes looked...scared. That was the face of a terrified man, and it nearly broke her heart.

"What are you doing?" she called through the window.

He flicked his hand as if to tell her to go away. Right, like that was happening.

"What's wrong?" she asked, exaggerating her mouth so he could read her lips.

He shook his head. "Go, Beck. Just go."

She put her hand on the handle and tried to open it, but it was locked. "I'm not leaving you here, Bill. There's a hurricane coming. What's wrong with you?"

Suddenly, the window came down slowly, removing the barrier and letting her see his ravaged expression.

"Everything," he said on a ragged whisper. "Everything is wrong."

The rain poured over her head and face, but she refused to move.

"How can I help you?" she said, reaching into the truck to put a hand on his shoulder.

The gesture seemed to break him, making his face collapse with a heart-wrenching sob. "I'm in so much trouble, Beck. I don't know how anyone can help me."

"Try me." It sounded like a challenge because it was one, enough to pull the slightest smile from his lips.

"You're so strong, Beck, you know that?"

"Then tell me what you need and let me help you."

His eyes squeezed closed as if the response just did him in. "How did you get this strong?" he asked, musing like she wasn't standing there in the pouring rain looking like a drowned rat with streaky mascara. "Was it having a baby as a teenager?" he asked. "Was it that tough-as-nails Olivia, the mother that wasn't your mother? Did she make you this strong?"

"Bill, I—"

"It's what's had me attracted to you from the moment I got here, did you know that? Life doesn't fold you in half. It doesn't scare you. You don't need to...numb the pain or hide from reality."

She remembered his ex-wife then, and suspected that's what really was at the core of his heartache. "Listen, why don't we—"

"And you know what else you don't need?"

What she needed was an umbrella, but now she knew better than to say a word. Whatever he had to get out, it was going to be now, in the rain, to a captive audience. Maybe that was the way she could help him.

"You don't need a man to solve your problems," he continued. "You face them down, figure them out, and carry on. If you didn't have the money to make this a B&B?" He gave a vague gesture to the house behind her. "Why, you'd just come up with plan B. You'd tap into your storehouse of personal power and figure it out. You'd never drink yourself into oblivion or endanger someone else's life or get yourself to..." A sob threatened and she reached into the truck again.

"Natalie?" She didn't care that he would find out she knew his personal business; he needed help.

"I had to get her into a program that would work, Beck." He stabbed his thick, silver hair and dragged it back. "She's going to kill herself or someone else. I'm the one who had to do it. And I did, but..."

"What happened?" She was almost afraid to ask.

"I did a really dumb, dumb thing."

"You robbed Peter to pay Paul?"

"Peter Granger," he said. "How's that for irony? And he wants his money back and I don't freaking have it because I used it to pay for the first month of a rehab facility in Atlanta that is Natalie's last chance."

"And he won't give you more time?"

"Apparently not." He squeezed his eyes like a wave of pain had rolled over him. "And I tried to...convince you to spend more. I was going to use that draw," he admitted on an aching whisper. "I was going to use your money to save my ass."

"Because your wife's in trouble."

"Ex-wife, and...I'm so..." He sobbed again, letting his

head drop. "I'm so ashamed. I tried to...charm it out of you. I would have paid you back, obviously, but I knew with you, and Kenny, I'd have time and forgiveness. Now I don't have either one."

"Oh, Bill." She squeezed his shoulder. "You have my forgiveness."

"How?" he shot back. "It's pathetic. I'm pathetic."

The words shredded her heart. "Pathetic? For wanting to take care of the woman you were married to, the mother of your children? You're pathetic for putting your life on hold and trying to figure out a solution to the problem you created because you wanted to save her life?"

"She needs help so bad, Beck," he rasped. "I had to do something."

"Of course you did. And now, you have to figure out how to pay that debt."

"Not by convincing you to do some dumb grand suite," he said, almost smiling. "That was a wretched plan."

"But we all can help you come up with a better one. We can help you because you just need money and time to pay it back. Anything that can be solved with money isn't a problem, it's just a challenge. Kenny will help you, and so will I."

He stared at her for a long time, a storm of emotions brewing in his eyes with the same strength as the one barreling through the Atlantic.

"Rebecca Mitchell," he whispered.

"Billy Dobson," she replied with a smile.

"You know what I thought the first time I saw you?"

"How can I get her into the back seat of my Camaro?"

He smiled. "The second first time, right here, in front of the house. I thought that I should make you fall in love with me, marry you, and then the night before our wedding, we could sit Ava down and tell her we're her grandparents."

She just stared at him, the fantasy so romantic, it made her heart slide around. "Oh, Bill."

"But that's never gonna happen because I'm a schmuck who took the easy way and tried to steal your money instead of your heart."

She gave his shoulder a squeeze. "You didn't steal either one, and we're going to help you out of this situation. I'm going to run in the house because Ava thinks she left her flat iron on. Then I'll leave my car and drive with you back to Kenny's house. We'll all hunker down safely."

He sighed with enough resignation for her to know she'd won.

"And please text Kenny," she added. "He's been worried sick about you."

"Why?"

"Bill! You've been missing for days."

"I've been holed up with friends in Key West. But I meant why would you do this for me?"

"Family," she said softly. "We are family."

Five minutes later, with the flat iron unplugged and her car safely in the carport, Beck climbed into the passenger seat and they left. She squeezed the water out of her hair while Bill drove in what felt like a peaceful silence.

As they pulled up to Kenny's house, she was surprised to see another truck had taken her parking spot in the driveway. The rain had let up enough for her to get a good look at it and the man climbing out of the front when Bill parked on the street.

Josh was here!

Before she could reach for the handle to jump out and greet him, Bill wrapped his arm around her and pulled her in for a long, strong hug.

"I don't know how to thank you, Beck."

She knew—let her get out and run to Josh, because her whole body felt lighter and joyous at the sight of him.

"It's fine," she said. "I'm so glad I went back to the house and found you."

He drew back and put his hands on her cheeks and for one minute, she really thought he was going to kiss her. And she did not want that. Not with Josh standing there, not ever, not at all.

"Thank you," he whispered again.

"Go in and see Kenny. He's anxious to see you."

Finally he released her, and she whipped around to see Josh, who'd turned from Bill's truck and seemed busy getting something out of the back of his.

"Joshua Cross!" She practically danced up the driveway, vaguely aware that Bill had headed toward the house, and Kenny had come out to greet him.

But her attention was laser-focused on the man she didn't realize she'd missed to the point of tears...like the ones springing to her eyes right now.

It was *so good* to see him. So wonderful to look into the blue eyes of a man who was rock steady and made of pure goodness.

No, he wasn't the handsome charmer that Bill Dobson was, but he was the very best kind of man, maybe the best she'd ever met.

"I didn't mean to interrupt that..." He notched his head toward Bill's truck. "Kiss."

"No, no you didn't...it wasn't...no." She reached his side and ached to throw her arms around him, but he looked...hurt. Betrayed. Uncertain. And *wrong*.

Hadn't someone just told Beck how very strong she was? It was time to tap into some of that strength right now.

"You misread the situation," she said firmly.

He threw a look at Bill who was just disappearing into the house with Kenny. "Did I?" He sounded more hopeful than skeptical.

She grabbed the sleeve of his T-shirt and yanked him around to face her. "What are you doing here?"

"I didn't want you to go through your first hurricane alone, Beck, but you're not, so—"

She reached up, got on her toes, and pulled him by the shoulders to her. "I missed you," she whispered, closing her eyes and punctuating that with a kiss.

He froze at first, then smiled under her lips, then she felt his hands come around her waist to tighten the hug and deepen the kiss.

"Yeah," he said when they finally broke, his voice somehow gruff and warm. "Same."

CHAPTER TWENTY
KENNY

*K*enny might never have been in a hurricane before, but between the graphics on TV showing just how close the storm was, and the howling winds, groaning branches, and constant thunder, he could tell they were getting slammed. The eye might not be hitting Coconut Key, but the son of a gun would *not* turn north. A front kept the whole storm on a path to South Florida, which wasn't the worst possible scenario for the Keys, but it wasn't good.

Had he nailed those protective boards well enough for Coquina House? That third floor wasn't built with block and a small tornado whipping through could do some major damage. And Lovely's little cottage? Would that roof hold? Would the shutters on this house be enough? Was that creaking sound the rafters about to lift?

At three AM, questions plagued while he walked the house, imagining what this island looked like outside of the cocoon he'd built for family and friends. He'd made the rounds about twenty times now, with the hearty little terrier, Pepper, who must have been a first responder in another life.

Trees were no doubt down all over the island, and power outages had to be rampant. The power had flickered a few times in the house, but it hung on for the moment while torrential rain battered against the metal shutters that covered his windows. When the power went out, which he knew it would, he'd have no way to get outside to the generator. It would be hot, airless, and pitch black when that happened, but he had plenty of flashlights on hand.

In the living room, Beck slept on the sofa with Peyton nearby on a blow-up mattress. Maybe they slept. The TV was on without sound and he thought he heard them whispering, but they were quiet when he walked through, doing his "rounds" of the house that hadn't even had a chance to become a home.

Lovely had gone into the tiny guest room with the other two dogs, and Ava had insisted Savannah sleep on her bed, with Ava on the floor.

Josh was snoring softly in the recliner, which left Bill, who was sitting in the kitchen staring into a cup of coffee that had long gone cold. After he got back, Bill had taken Kenny aside and told him everything. He'd made some rash and expensive decisions, but was firm in his belief that Natalie would finally have a chance at this rehab center.

The only problem was, Peter Granger wanted his money...and Bill couldn't get his hands on that kind of cash without a big job. A major one. And even then, he'd be doing the same thing...using his draw on one project to pay off a different one.

The fact was, Bill could go to jail for what he'd done if someone pushed...and Granger was just pushy enough to scare him. So, he'd spent a few weeks being "unavailable" by hiding out in Coconut Key...and maybe using the time to try and persuade Beck to hand him that "big" job.

He knew it had been wrong on every level, and his miserable expression reflected that.

"All quiet on the western front?" Bill asked.

"Nothing's broken, roof's intact, and most everyone is asleep or trying." He poured himself a cup of coffee and took it to the table, sitting down across from Bill. "How are you?"

He just snorted. "It's good to have this crap off my chest."

"What can we do?"

Bill looked up, his dark eyes softening. "Just the fact that you asked that, and Beck offered? You've done more than I deserve. Look, I'll head back to Atlanta when this storm passes and face Granger. I'll buy some time, see if I can pick up some more work." He tunneled his fingers into his hair and dragged it back. "But I don't want to leave Beck in the lurch."

"Beck will have a job for you to GC, Bill. But I don't want you using her draw to pay a dime to Granger. You have to do this the legit way."

"God, I know." He put his elbows on the table and leaned in. "I've been thinking about something. Feel free to say no, but—"

"No." Kenny smiled over his cup. "Just kidding. What do you need?"

"For Ava to know the truth."

Kenny looked at him, not surprised, for some reason.

"I didn't think it mattered," Bill continued. "And it's totally your call, but I've just been sitting here thinking about...family. Whatever the size and shape and history, Beck made me realize that connections with family are vital. They're what life is, you know?"

He nodded. "You're telling a man who has lost four of his favorite family members, Bill. No one knows the value of family like I do. We can tell her."

"But here's the thing," Bill said. "Here's where you might say no. I'd like to tell her myself."

Kenny studied him, considering the request.

"She's not as tender or volatile as she was in Atlanta," he continued. "She's settled here, with aunts and a grandmother who adore her. I think she can handle it."

"I agree," Kenny said. "When you first got here, I was on the fence about it. But knowing you're my biological father is grounding to me. Knowing you're her grandfather will likely be the same." He grimaced. "I hope."

"She might be ticked off at us for keeping the secret," Bill said, "but she's not a baby anymore. I'd like her to know the truth. And if I don't do it alone, that's fine. But I want to be next to her when she finds out."

Kenny nodded, at peace with that decision.

"Daddy?"

He turned to see Ava, her hair a mess, her shoulders hunched as she hugged herself around a baggy T-shirt and sleep pants covered in bright pink flowers. For a moment, he wondered if she'd heard the conversation, but she looked way more terrified than shocked to have heard.

"What's up, A?" he asked.

"I'm really scared." Her voice cracked and he was up instantly to put his arms around her.

"Oh, baby, we're gonna be fine."

"It's loud. And close. On the news they said it's tearing Fort Lauderdale to pieces. That's way further south than we thought. And what about Aunt Katherine? She lives really close to the water."

"I talked to her earlier," he said. "She left days ago and went to her sister's in Dallas. And"—he added a teasing smile—"since you broke all the rules and left your Aunt Katherine's house and took an Uber from Ft. Lauderdale to Coconut Key? You know how far that storm really is."

"Two hours and forty minutes," she said. "And *so* much money."

"That you will pay me back, Missy." He gave her a playful squeeze. "But you should know that it's far enough that we're not going to get wiped out by winds or rain. We might have some damage, trees will be down, power will probably go out."

A rolling bolt of thunder shook the house as if to underscore what he was saying, followed by a quick flicker of the lights, making Ava gasp.

"It sounds so awful!"

"Shhh." He stroked her hair. "Is Savannah doing okay?"

"She's asleep but she keeps moaning. She's louder than the storm."

"You wanna sleep in my bed?" Kenny asked. "I'm not going to be anywhere near it tonight. Why don't you try it, Goldilocks?"

She smiled at a nickname he hadn't used on her in years.

"Okay." But she didn't sound convinced, only terrified and so, so young despite her sixteen years, pink and purple hair, and that driver's license she was so proud of.

"Come on. I'll tuck you in."

He fully expected an eye roll and a "get real" look, but she surprised him by calling out a good night to Bill and letting him lead her down the hall to his room while, overhead, he heard the trusses creaking again.

"Did you hear that?" She froze as they walked into his room. "Is the roof coming off?"

"Nope." At least he hoped not. He led her to the bed and pulled back the covers. "The roof is just fine, I promise you. It's just a little give in the rafters, some wind under the shingles. This is a heavy band, but it'll be over soon."

She crawled in and pulled the covers all the way under her chin, looking up at him. "I miss Mommy tonight."

His heart folded in half as he perched on the edge of the bed. "I do, too, honey. I miss her every day and every night."

"But you have Maggie now."

He felt his mouth pull in a humorless expression. "We're, um, not, seeing each other anymore."

"Oh." She sat up, bracing on her elbows. "It's not because of me, is it?"

"Absolutely not," he promised her. "We're just too different and it's not the right time."

"I get it." She eased back. "It's hard to replace Mom."

"I will *never* replace Mom," he said, leaning a little closer. "That woman was one in a million. You know she'd have made a full-blown hurricane party out of this."

"Yeah." Ava managed a weak smile. "She made things fun. She also made things...better. I mean when I was scared. But I was little."

"How did she do that?" he asked. "Because I need some help right now."

"Oh, she prayed."

He laughed softly, thinking about how in any situation, good or bad, Elise found a way to pray. If she were here, she'd have had everyone in this house gather before the first rain drop fell. She'd have figured out a way to thank Jesus for the storm, then she'd read a Bible verse about how it's all in His power. And she did it in such a genuine and honest way that people just...responded to her.

Why did God take one of his best emissaries so young? He rooted for his usual resentment, but tonight, none came.

"Praying was how she magically took away all the scariness of life, Dad," Ava's voice was thick with emotion.

"It wasn't magic," he said, putting the heel of his hand over his breastbone because it felt heavy or empty in there. "It was her strong, unwavering faith."

Another gust howled outside along with a deep, deep rumble of thunder, making the storm shutters on his windows shake and squeak. Ava clutched at the comforter and let out a whimper as he moved closer.

"I'm so scared of this hurricane," she whispered. "I just have a really bad feeling."

"Honey, we're all going to be fine." He smoothed her

hair, digging for the words or ways to make her feel better, the way Elise would. "Do you want to...pray?"

She blinked at him. "You don't pray anymore."

"But I didn't forget how," he said. "You said that's what Mom would do."

"Yeah, and read the Bible. She would definitely read the Bible." She closed her eyes for a moment. "She'd say, 'Ava Bear, this calls for a little ninety-one.' I don't know what that means, but then she'd read something, and I felt better."

He knew what it meant. Psalm 91. Definitely one of Elise's go-to scriptures when times got tough.

"Well, I could...read that to you."

"You have a Bible?" She seemed stunned by that.

"I have your mother's Bible." Hadn't cracked it in five years, but he knew where it was. "Do you want me to read that ninety-one to you?"

She sat up, the storm temporarily forgotten. "Yes, please."

He pushed off the bed and went to the closet, where he'd put a box of Elise's belongings that he'd been carting from one rental to the next. He hadn't gone through it in a long time, but he knew her Bible was in there.

Right on top, in fact.

His hands closed over the worn navy blue leather, his thumb grazing her name embossed in gold script along the bottom right corner.

Taking a deep breath, he pulled it out and headed back to the bed, where Ava had scooted over and offered a pillow for him to lean on against the headboard.

"Thank you, Dad," she said softly, sliding down under the covers.

"Sure thing." His fingers felt big and clumsy over the pages as he opened the book, his gaze instantly falling on some writing in the margin. Lots of writing. Different colors. Highlighted sections. A heart, an exclamation point, a date.

Elise didn't just read a Bible, she rolled around in it.

He flipped through the Old Testament, pausing at the pages of pink highlighter in the book of Ruth. She always liked that one, he remembered. Called it "a romance novel" in the middle of the Bible.

"Here we go, Psalm 91," he said.

Ava let her head fall against his arm, relaxed for the first time. "Does it start with 'Whoever dwells in the shadow...' or something?"

"The shelter," he corrected without thinking about it. "'Whoever dwells in the shelter of the Most High.'"

"Yes!" She beamed up at him. "That's it. That's the one."

Another screaming gust of wind shook the shutter and made the roof groan, making Ava burrow deeper.

He cleared his throat and took a breath, his gaze sliding down the margin to the words *You will not fear the terror of night, nor the arrow that flies by day.* She'd underlined *nor the pestilence that stalks in the darkness.* Next to that, Elise had printed *Adam, March 14, 2013.*

Oh, yes. He remembered the day very well. Their son, then three years old, had been taken to the hospital with a respiratory virus that had scared the daylights out of them.

Kenny's mother had come to the hospital and brought this Bible. Elise read it for hours next to Adam's bed, frequently on her knees until their baby's lungs had cleared.

"Go ahead, Dad."

He swallowed, not at all sure he could talk. Nothing could convince Elise that Adam's life hadn't been saved by God's hand.

"'kay. Here we go. 'Whoever dwells in the shelter of the Most High will rest in the shadow of the Almighty.'"

"I knew there was a shadow in it," Ava murmured, her eyes closed. "Keep reading."

He did, slowly speaking the words that, if he really wanted to, he could close his eyes and recite. Maybe not perfectly like Elise, but he knew this psalm. He knew its power. He knew its strength. He knew the peace that came with every word.

"'For He will command his angels concerning you,'" he whispered, the words blurred by tears he didn't want or understand. "'To guard you in all your ways.'"

Was Elise up there, guarding him? He knew enough about this book he held to know she didn't "turn into heaven's newest angel" when she died, and neither did Adam. But they were...somewhere. And they had to be happy, right? Hadn't she fervently believed that was the truth?

And hadn't Kenny believed that, too, way back when? Did faith just disappear? Could it come back? Or maybe it had never really left.

He pushed the thought away and kept reading, glancing at Ava when he finished. Her eyes were closed and her chest rose and fell with even breaths, asleep. Calm and at peace.

He started to close the book but stopped, dragging his

gaze back to the last lines of the scripture, reading it one more time. But this time, the words seemed to move on the page with...life. They were real. They were *true*. And something in him wanted to read them out loud again, slowly and deliberately.

"'He will call on me, and I will answer him. I will be with him in trouble, I will deliver him and honor him. With long life I will satisfy him and show him my salvation.'" He looked up at the ceiling. "Really? Will You do that? Deliver and honor...and all I have to do is call on You...again?"

He blinked and swiped the tear that trickled down his cheek. Could he do that? Could he forgive God for taking away Elise and Adam? Could he—

"Kenny! Kenny!" Beck's voice, taut with panic, made him slam the Bible closed and wake Ava, both of them sitting up as Beck whipped around the doorway, breathless.

"What's wrong?" He was up in an instant.

"Savannah." She pressed her hand on her chest, her eyes swimming with tears. "Her water broke. She's going into labor."

"What?" Ava shrieked, but Kenny bolted out the door, tearing down the small hall to Ava's room.

There, Savannah sat up in the bed, her hair wild, her eyes wilder. "Can you really deliver a baby?" she asked in a ragged, broken whisper. "'Cause it feels like this guy is coming...soon."

He was vaguely aware of the group gathering behind him, questions and comments and exclamations spilling out as he forced himself to focus and dig for all his training and baby delivery experience. "How far apart are the contractions?"

"A couple minutes? Two or three? I mean, they've been happening all day but—"

"You didn't say anything?" That was Beck, echoing what everyone in the room and hall was thinking.

"They weren't that serious. Just Braxton Hicks stuff. But..." She dropped her head back and grimaced in pain. "This might be the real deal."

"Josh, call 911 and tell them we need an ambulance for a premature delivery, stat," Kenny said.

"Will they come?" Beck asked.

"Maybe. Depends on what their no-go threshold is and if the roads are clear. Just get them on the phone and I'll talk to dispatch. They'll have every first responder on duty tonight, so just pray they have an ambulance available." And pray they aren't dealing with a bunch of fallen trees or drunk partiers or, God forbid, a house fire from a crappy generator. "Beck, get a phone and start timing contractions. You'll stay in the room with me. Everyone else, get out."

"But, Dad—"

"Out!" Just then the lights flickered once, then twice. And then they went out completely.

Ava shrieked and Bill swore and Savannah groaned like someone was tearing her insides out.

"Get me all the flashlights in the house!" Kenny ordered, making his way toward the bed and reaching out to find Savannah's hand in the pitch black room. "You're going to be okay, Savannah. I promise."

"But is my baby? It's three weeks early! My placenta is torn! This is bad, Kenny."

"Shhh." He calmed her in the same voice he'd just used with Ava, maybe a little less confident this time. A lot less. "As soon as I can see, I'm gonna look. You okay with that?"

"Are you kidding? Just save my baby!" she cried.

He closed his eyes and tried to prepare for the delivery he hoped to God he didn't have to do.

God. Him again.

He will call on me and I will answer him. I will be with him in trouble. I will deliver him.

The words of the scripture he'd just read echoed in his head, louder than the rain, wind, or Savannah's cries.

Okay, You win. This is me calling. Please answer...and deliver.

CHAPTER TWENTY-ONE
BECK

"Breathe, Savannah. Breathe." Beck smoothed the three towels she placed under Savannah since they couldn't get the bed changed without moving her and Kenny didn't want to risk that. "Like they told us in that class."

"Stupid class. They didn't tell us it would happen during a hurricane."

"I did," Kenny said, pressing the phone to his ear. "Barometric pressure."

The dispatcher at 911 couldn't promise an ambulance for a while. Several trees were down blocking main roads, and there were calls coming in fast and furious. Kenny had gotten them on the list for help and started digging through the process of calling the closest fire station directly.

That took quite a bit of time, during which the contractions got closer and more intense. Beck didn't know if hours or minutes had past, since her entire concentration was on timing the contractions and supporting her daughter.

"Yes, is this the station manager?"

Finally, he got through to someone.

"My name is Ken Gallagher, I'm with Station 468 in the Atlanta area..." He walked out of the room, his voice low and serious, everyone trying like hell to protect Savannah from whatever she needed to be protected from.

Beck tamped down the most wretched fear she'd ever known and refused to think about Savannah having this baby—the one so delicately held in place—tonight, in this house, during a hurricane, with no power, no doctor, no equipment, and no hope.

She shook off the thought. She couldn't lose hope.

"He's so still," Savannah rasped. "Mom, why is he so still? I'm scared."

She had no idea why, but she stroked Savannah's arm. "Breathe."

"Do better than that," Savannah ordered, probably not even kidding. "Was I still during labor? Peyton or Callie?"

"I don't remember. Callie came on her due date, though."

Savannah managed a bark of a laugh. "Of course she did. In sensible work shoes, ready to bill hours."

The words were a balm on Beck's pounding heart. If Savannah was joking, she couldn't be that bad, right?

"I know Kenny's going to get an ambulance here."

Savannah responded by squeezing Beck's hand. "Can you call Nick for me?"

"You want to talk to him now?"

"Shouldn't he know I'm in labor? I mean, he's called me six times today to check in on the...storm..." She grunted out the last few words, almost impossible to understand with the howling wind and rain outside.

"Another one?"

"Not yet. I'm just..." She turned her head from one side to the other. "I miss him. How dumb is that?"

"It's not dumb at all. You know he was going to move heaven and earth to be here on your due date."

"Why? Why does he care? Why do I?"

Beck smoothed Savannah's hair, not surprised her brow was wet from sweating through the last contraction. Plus, the AC went out with the power, so it was stifling hot in this house.

"Shhh. Save your strength for the next contraction," Beck said.

"Which is starting in five...four...three...oh, God this is awful."

Beck checked the phone. One minute apart. She might not remember all the details of delivery, but she knew it was darn near go time.

Savannah groaned through the pain, which Beck would have given her right arm to take away. She remembered contractions—most women did. She remembered her skin and muscles feeling like two people were yanking her whole body in different directions.

"Better?" she asked as it ended and Savannah released the grip that had her nails digging into Beck's palm. "By the way, that was one minute apart. We have to get you to the hospital."

"They're on their way." Kenny marched into the room

sounding both frustrated and relieved. "It's just taking a long time."

"Trees down?" Beck asked.

"And two strokes, one heart attack, and a moron who left his car running in the garage and damn near killed a houseful of people with carbon monoxide."

Beck gasped.

"Yeah. The baby is a little lower on their list, but I managed to explain the placenta situation and they are sending over their best team and bringing a portable Neonatal ICU."

Beck's eyes shuttered closed as it hit her again and again how truly fragile this baby's life was.

Savannah sobbed as if she had the very same thought.

"Hush, sweetie," Beck said. "You're about to have another contraction."

"But why isn't he moving?" Savannah asked, blinking back tears. "Could he have..."

"Stop it, Savannah," Beck warned.

Kenny came closer to her. "Does the pressure seem lower?" he asked.

"Yeah, very low."

"And your breathing isn't quite so difficult."

She nodded. "It's better."

"You're getting close, kid," he said, his voice tight despite an effort to sound casual. "I left every piece of medical equipment in Atlanta. I wish I had a blood pressure monitor."

"I wish you had an epidural."

He put his hand on her shoulder. "You're making jokes, Savannah. That's a good sign."

"Oh...oh...what's this?" Savannah tried to sit up. "This is a new pain. This is different."

"What is it?" Beck asked, fighting the panic that tried to creep into her voice.

"Pressure. Like a fist...oh my God!" She threw her head back. "I have to push!"

No! Beck looked at Kenny, who was already moving into position, pulling down the bed clothes and grabbing a flashlight. "Put your legs up, Savannah. Let me see if the baby's crowning."

How could that be? Was it because of the placenta problem? Beck got right in Savannah's face, as close as she could, holding both hands while Kenny did the exam.

"Just breathe, baby. Don't think. Don't spiral. Just—"

"Oh, man," Kenny said. "He's knockin' at the door." He looked up at Beck, his eyes dark with the seriousness of the situation, which he obviously didn't want to tell Savannah, whose eyes were closed as she fought not to push.

"Now?" she mouthed.

"Soon," he replied.

Fear strangled her, but she refused to give in to it. "Okay. We can do this."

"They're here!" Peyton's voice broke through all the noise of the storm and Savannah's groans. "The ambulance is here! We heard the siren!"

"Oh, thank God." Beck nearly collapsed.

"Get them back here this minute," Kenny barked the order. "And bring the stretcher, oxygen, and the portable incubator, and..." He stopped for a minute. "I'll deal with them. Savannah, do not push this baby out yet!"

He shot out of the room and Peyton replaced him, taking the other side of the bed.

"Is it that close?" she asked, fear darkening her voice.

"So close," Beck said.

Savannah reached out, grabbing each of their hands in hers. "If I die, please take care of my baby."

"Savannah, stop it!" Beck demanded.

"I'm serious, Mom. Pey, please. Please listen to me, you guys. If it's my life or his, there's no question, right? You understand that. He's way more important than I am, and you have to raise him. Both of you. And Lovely. Do not let Nick take him away to California. I don't care what he says and how much he claims to love this kid, I want him raised right here in Coconut Key with you. And his name is *not* Sebastian!"

Beck looked over at Peyton who had tears streaming down her face, and used her free hand to wipe some of her own.

"You're not going to die, Sav," Peyton insisted.

"Promise me, damn it! I need to know. And, oh my God, I need to push. Promise me, both of you!"

"We promise," Beck whispered, hearing the roar of wind and rain as someone opened the front door.

"We do," Peyton agreed.

"Coming in," Kenny called. "Clear out."

Peyton jumped up, but Beck leaned over and put one quick kiss on Savannah's damp forehead. "You can do this, Savannah Joy Foster. And you are going to be a stunning, wonderful mom and this baby is going to be healthy and perfect and the king of Coconut Key."

She looked up and managed a smile. "I love you, Mom."

"I love you, too."

And suddenly the room was filled with soaking wet first responders who filed in with a stretcher, an IV, oxygen, and an air of authority that gave Beck some measure of relief. She and Peyton slipped out between them, holding hands, heading back to the living room where everyone was gathered while Josh cleaned up the rainwater that had come in through the open door.

When he saw Beck, he abandoned the floor and went right to her, wrapping his arms around her and pulling her into his chest. Lovely and Ava sat arm in arm on the sofa with a book opened between them, Ava's cell phone flashlight shining on the pages.

Oh, not a book. *The* book. Apparently, Ava had produced a Bible.

Bill leaned against the dining room door jamb, quietly taking it all in.

"She could have this baby in your room, Ava," Beck said, sitting down on the sofa next to her.

"It's okay," Ava said, remarkably calm. "She's going to be okay. I just know it."

"I do, too," Beck put an arm around her and gave a squeeze. "You're going to be a great godmother."

They heard Savannah cry out and Beck bent over, letting the tears flow. Josh came over next to her to wrap her in a comforting hug. Outside, the wind seemed to hit its own crescendo, with flashes of lightning illuminating the room through the small window in the front door.

"It's making landfall in North Miami Beach," Bill announced, looking at his phone. "The worst damage is the north eye wall, but it's a big storm and we're going to see some damage in the Keys."

Beck watched Peyton press both hands over her mouth. Val Sanchez was in Miami, Beck remembered. "Have you heard from him?" Beck asked softly.

She turned and shook her head, her face still tearstained from the last conversation.

"He'll be fine," Beck assured her.

"We all will be," Lovely said. "We're Coconutters, right, Ava?"

Ava managed a soft laugh and put her head on Lovely's shoulder. "That's right. We are."

Suddenly, a high-pitched wail broke through all the noise, the sweet, soft cry of a brand-new baby. A cheer went up in the room from everyone but Beck, who stood and almost needed to be restrained to keep from running back there.

"Just wait," Josh said, holding her again. "Just breathe."

She wrapped her arms around him and pressed her face into his shoulder, fighting the tears and listening to the sound of the baby. Suddenly, Kenny came running down the hall.

"Everyone is fine," he called out. "We're taking them to the hospital. Clear a path and do not try to follow. Beck, you can ride in the ambulance with them."

"Oh, thank you!" She squeezed Josh's shoulders. "Did you hear? Fine. They're fine."

He just kissed her cheek and let her go.

"You'll need your sneakers, Mom." Peyton was next to her, holding them up.

"And your bag." Ava jumped up to get Beck's purse.

"Don't forget your phone!" Lovely added.

Beck stopped moving for one second to look at them

all with love, then three paramedics came down the hall with Savannah on a stretcher. Behind her was a second stretcher with a large white machine covered with acrylic —a portable incubator.

Inside the incubator, there was a tiny—oh, heavens, so small—unwashed newborn, who wiggled and writhed. They all watched in stunned silence as the baby wheeled by and the lead medic opened the door and led them out.

"You ready, Beck?" Kenny called.

She nodded and hustled closer.

"He's flawless," Kenny assured her. "Very, very small."

"And Savannah?"

He blinked back tears. "I'm so proud of my sister."

She wrapped her arm around him and ran into the storm.

CHAPTER TWENTY-TWO
KENNY

$\mathscr{H}$e knew by the time they'd crossed the mess that was US1 that the potential for damage on the beach was strong, but Kenny wasn't quite prepared for how hard Coquina Court got hit. The street that was home to Chuck's Restaurant, Lovely's cottage, and a budding B&B was strewn with palm fronds and branches, lined with some uprooted trees, and still under about an inch of water.

Coconut Key hadn't been obliterated, but the vulnerable ocean-front properties had been slammed.

The group drove over in a small caravan after dropping Josh at the hospital to be with Beck and Savannah. Kenny had talked to Beck early this morning and the report was good. The baby boy who Kenny had witnessed take his very first breath was barely five pounds, but his lungs were functioning in his incubator, and all the vital signs were good.

Savannah was in a room recovering and was on track

to be up and about in day or two, so they were all euphoric on that news.

Now to find out how badly damaged the properties were.

They had to take a few detours due to downed trees, but made it all the way to Chuck's without having to stop and move a tree on Coquina Court. At the restaurant, they found no major damage other than some missing shingles and a fallen live oak that had mercifully missed everything but the parking lot.

Inside, the restaurant had suffered from some significant leaks in the main dining room ceiling, but the boards held up on the windows and there was no flooding. All of the Keys had missed the storm surge, which was a blessing—since water, they all knew, could cause a heck of a lot more damage than wind.

"No one is eating in here for a while," Peyton said as she walked over some puddles on the hardwood and examined the huge water marks in the ceiling.

"A good water restoration team can fix that ceiling and make sure you don't get any mold. You'll be open in a month or so."

"What does that cost?" she asked, worried for Jessie.

"It costs the insurance deductible, which she has." Lovely slid a reassuring arm around Peyton. "And this isn't bad at all, thanks to Kenny's fantastic boarding up. You can be up and running soon, I think."

After checking the kitchen and doing a quick Face-Time to Jessie, they made their way down the road to Lovely's cottage, happy to see the storm hadn't done too much damage at first glance. But the joy dissipated when they went inside and discovered the roof missing in one section on the corner of the house, leaving the bedroom uninhabitable.

"You'll stay with us, Lovely," Kenny said as she stared up at the light coming through the ripped roof, and then plucked the soaking wet comforter covered with soggy insulation from her bed.

"We'll have slumber parties every night," Ava promised.

But Lovely just gave them a bittersweet smile. "Thank you and yes, we will, although not on school nights, young lady." She tapped Ava's nose. "I'm not fazed, in case you're wondering. I put my valuables in the safe room at Coquina House."

They dried everything as well as they could, moving the bed and laying down some plastic sheets Kenny had in his truck. Lovely packed what she needed and then they headed as a group to see Coquina House.

"Time to find out if our reno schedule changed," Kenny said as they started down the street, pausing to move some giant coconut palm fronds from the road.

A few minutes later, they were all standing on the veranda, staring up at...nothing. The entire east-facing wall of the third floor was gone.

"Well, demo's done," Bill said dryly.

"I knew those two-by-fours might not hold the third floor," Kenny said, shaking his head. "That was built before the codes were quite as stringent as they are now."

"That floor was added by my father," Lovely said. "How it managed to survive this long is a miracle. When you rebuild and restore, you'll make it stronger."

Kenny turned to her, amazed again at her calm and positive attitude. "You're taking this well, Lovely."

She lifted a shoulder. "Every single thing can be repaired, rebuilt, and fixed. And the inside of the house is perfect, not a single leak, even on the second floor, which is a testament to how this grand old dame is built."

As far as he was concerned, the grand old dame was the one he was looking at. "Good attitude, Lovely."

She reached out and took his hand and put her other arm around Ava, who'd been very quiet as they surveyed the damage. "What matters is family. That can't be replaced. Didn't we learn that last night?"

"I know," he said, his voice a little gruff.

"You're right, Lovely," Bill said, coming up on the other side. "I want to go check that shed, Ken. Ava, you want to come with me?"

"Sure."

Bill threw Kenny a meaningful look and Kenny knew exactly what the older man was trying to communicate. *Now? Can I?* And *Do you want to be there?*

He hadn't talked to Beck about it yet, but Kenny's gut told him that Beck would have no issues with the revelation. Telling her first was a courtesy, but she was so happy right now, it seemed crazy to wait. After what they'd all been through and how it all could have been so much worse, forty-year-old secrets seemed silly.

He gave a nearly imperceptible nod, and instantly Bill guided Ava around the stairs.

"Let's get off this veranda, Lovely," Kenny said, following her with Peyton. "Just until I can do a thorough inspection."

At the bottom, Peyton and Lovely walked toward the beach and Kenny almost accompanied them to see how the tide had affected everything. But he saw Ava and Bill walking and talking and he knew he should be there to catch her if she fell.

Just as they reached the shed, Bill stopped and turned to Ava, who looked up at him with an expectant expression.

"Uncle Bill says he has something important to tell me," she said to Kenny as he joined them.

"He does."

She frowned and looked from one to the other. "What's going on, you two?"

Bill glanced at him, but Kenny tipped his head to let him do the honors.

After a second, Bill put his hands on her shoulders and looked down at her. "I have some news."

"Are you leaving?" She sounded truly disappointed. "I mean, I know something's going on with all the hushy grown-up discussions last night, but I don't want you to leave, Uncle Bill."

"I'm not...your uncle."

She snorted a laugh. "I know that."

"I'm your...grandfather."

"Oh, so you want me to call you Grandpa now..." Her voice and smile faded as the words sunk in. "What?" She looked up at Kenny. "What's he talking about?"

"Ava, you know how Beck is my biological mother who gave me up for adoption?" Kenny asked.

"Yes?"

"Well, Bill is..." He didn't finish on purpose, waiting for her to put it all together.

And when her eyes flashed, he knew she had. She took a step backwards, her complexion paling a little.

"You mean you...and Beck...and Dad...and..." She shook her head. "You're Dad's father?"

Bill nodded. "We're sorry we never told you. We've never told anyone, but when you found Beck and everything came out, then..."

She held up one hand, the other on her chest. "Wait. Wait. *Wait*." For a second, it looked like she couldn't breathe as she blinked back tears. "Are you telling me that you are my actual and real grandfather?"

"I am," Bill said, looking as uncertain as Kenny felt.

"So I have a living grandfather and grandmother again?" Her voice rose with what could only be interpreted as excitement and...happiness? She was happy?

"You're not mad?" Bill asked, as confused as Kenny.

"Mad?" She choked a few times in disbelief. "Are you kidding me? Uncle Bill!" She threw her arms around him in the most insane hug Kenny could ever remember seeing Ava give to anyone. "Or should I say Grandpa? Gramps? Papa? What do you want me to call you?"

"Overjoyed," he murmured, hugging her again and looking over her head at Kenny, who probably had a pretty stupid grin on his face.

"Daddy!" She turned and reached for Kenny. "I have grandparents again!"

"You're really not upset that we didn't tell you?"

"Um...not really," she said, thinking about it. "I get all the secretive stuff. Beck told me about her mother and how she made people sign stuff. It was all hush-hush back then when it was frowned upon to have a baby at sixteen."

"It's *still* frowned upon," Kenny reminded her.

She just laughed and looked at Bill. "So you and Beck

were my age and..." She cringed. "Ew. Not going there. But I am going to tell Lovely. Can I?"

"She knows," Bill said. "She's the only person here who does besides us."

"I want to tell everyone," she exclaimed. "I love you, Uncle—Grandpa." Just saying it made her giggle. "And now you'll stay, right? Because you're family! You have to stay."

"Oh, honey," he said. "I got a heap of trouble to handle back in Atlanta."

"But you will," she said with the confidence of a kid who didn't know how high that heap was. "I just know you will. Do you and Beck...like each other again?"

"We're just friends," he said quickly. "And working together. But, nothing else."

"I really hope you stay here," she said. "Or visit all the time. I don't know why, but I really like you being my family."

"I know why," he said, his voice thick with emotion. "'Cause you're the best kid in the world." He hugged her again. "And I like being your family, too."

Grinning, she pointed to the house. "Can I tell everyone who'll listen?"

Bill blinked at her, his eyes damp. "Go forth and tell, kid."

She started to back away, blew them a double-handed air kiss, and took off, suddenly reminding Kenny so much of Elise, it hurt.

Bill huffed out a breath of pure relief watching her go. "Ya never know with that kid, do you?"

"I actually think the real Ava is emerging more every day."

"Somebody better warn Beck that we let the cat out of the bag," Bill added. "Thanks for letting me seize that moment. It just felt right."

"I'm texting Beck now," Kenny said, glancing at his phone. "I've been sending her pictures of the house."

"Is she okay?" Bill asked. "Upset about the third floor?"

"I don't think anything could upset her today." After hitting send, he looked up to find Bill on his phone, shaking his head. "Everything okay?" Kenny asked. "It's not Granger again, is it?"

"No, no." He angled the phone to read easier. "It's... holy heck. Three different people looking for a GC in the Keys. And one in South Florida." His face broke into a huge grin. "There's work from the storm," he said. "A metric buttload of work."

"Enough to pay your debts?"

He nodded, still reading. "Yes, I think so. There is going to be a mad scramble for licensed contractors after this storm."

"Then this can be your home base, Bill," Kenny said, catching the excitement because this was an answer to Bill's prayers. Insurance companies paid quickly and well, and he'd have enough work to pay that debt in a month or so. "Might get crowded at my house since I have a feeling Beck isn't staying at Coquina House, and it isn't going to be easy to get rental space for Peyton and Savannah and a baby, but we'll make do."

"Thank you." He lowered the phone and wiped a tear from his eye, relief carved all over his expression. "I love you, son. I really do."

Kenny pulled him into a hug, giving his back a solid

thump. "I love you..." He swallowed against an unexpected lump in his throat. "Dad."

"Oh, boy." Bill snorted an awkward laugh. "Now we've really lost it."

Chuckling, they headed back to the house, the sound of Ava's excited voice floating from the front of the house. Bill hustled forward but Kenny held back, listening to the conversation and letting his gaze travel over the broken branches, a few uprooted trees, and mess of a beach that had been under a significant amount of water the night before.

But the storm was gone, and there were blue skies above.

"Dad! Daddy!" Ava cried, coming around the house waving her phone. "You're not going to believe this!"

Right now, he'd believe anything.

"Savannah named the baby Dylan! Like the storm. She said it's a reminder that no matter what life throws at them, they will survive!"

He had to smile. "Perfect."

"And they said he can come home in a few days!"

Kenny closed his eyes, an old familiar feeling washing over him. Gratitude? Relief? Even a sense of freedom. Yes, it was all those things, but it was something else too...

Faith.

He squinted up to the sunny skies and whispered, "Thank you, Father. Thank you." And for the first time in five years, he had no doubt that prayer was heard.

CHAPTER TWENTY-THREE

SAVANNAH

"*S*omehow, my darling baby boy, it seems appropriate that I'm taking you to a temporary home." Savannah stroked the precious cheek of the tiniest human she'd ever seen, a five-day-old miracle who never failed to amaze her. "But that might be life with me, your tumbleweed of a mother."

He nestled closer to her breast as Savannah closed her eyes and leaned back on the rocker, somehow oddly used to this small private room attached to the newborn ICU. She'd spent a lot of time in here over the past few days, sleeping, learning how to breastfeed, and worrying about the future.

But when this wee creature opened his deep blue eyes and looked up into hers, all worry disappeared. They had each other and that was all they needed.

She rocked them both gently, glancing at the door when she heard footsteps, hoping it was the discharge nurse with the final papers.

But it was Beck Foster looking like the most radiant grandmother in the world as she greeted them both.

"How's my grandson doing? Does he know it's homecoming day?"

"I was just telling him. Trust me, he doesn't care where we live as long as I bring the sauce."

"Well, then I'll tell you the good news."

"Peyton found us all a rental?"

Mom's face fell as she sat in the chair across from Savannah.

"There's not an apartment, town house, or home to be had on Coconut Key," she said. "Everything was scooped up the day of the storm by people displaced on the beach, but there is good news. Kenny finished assembling the crib and I just bought a month's worth of diapers and as soon as you're settled, we'll have that baby shower for you."

"It's fine, Mom. Nothing about this baby from conception to birth has been traditional. Why start now?" She eased him away and slid her bra back on and nursing top into place. Still handling him like he was made of thin glass, she eased him up so he could rest his little head on her shoulder. "Just you for the big ride home?"

"You're kidding, right?" She laughed. "You're going in my car, where we'll put the car seat." She gestured toward the carrier on the table. "And you can sit in the back with him. Peyton, Ava, and Lovely will be behind us with Ava at the wheel of your car. Kenny and Josh are in the truck. Am I missing anyone?"

Savannah blinked back a sudden rush of tears, which actually didn't surprise her anymore. She could cry at anything these days, and frequently did.

"Nick," she whispered on a rough breath. "I really thought he'd try and find a way to come, but he said they're still shooting pick-ups from the last episode."

"Oh, honey. I'm sure he'll be here when he can."

"But not in time to take the baby home from the hospital. It's just kind of sad to miss that moment."

"He's going to miss a lot of moments unless you—"

Savannah lifted her hand from Dylan's back and held it up to her mom. "Stop. I'm not going to California. I've told him that, but to be fair, he hasn't really pushed. I think now that the baby's born, the novelty has worn off."

"Somehow I doubt that," Mom said.

"I don't know." Savannah sniffed back another onslaught of emotions. "It doesn't matter. I have my little pickle." She kissed his head and adjusted the tiny blue cap. "Dyl Pickle."

"You know that's going to stick," Mom joked. "Do you want your son to be called Dyl Pickle?"

She fought a smile, but it dissolved into tears again because...hormones. "I wanted him—and me—to have that moment of coming home from the hospital as a, you know...unit."

Mom sighed and leaned closer. "Savannah, when I had my one and only son, he was taken from me and given to another woman before I ever got to hold him, kiss him, feed him, or love him. I'm not looking for sympathy," she added quickly. "It was right at the time, and now that I know him, I am certain it was always right. But you *have* your baby."

"Thanks to that same son of yours," Savannah added. "How's that for poetic and circular irony and coolness?"

"It's all those things," her mother agreed. "But today

should be a happy day. If anything, I'm the one who's sad because my house got wrecked and you're going to a guest room in a place that isn't home, no matter how hard Kenny tries to make it so. And I should have had a baby shower."

"Where would we put all that stuff?" Savannah asked. "Don't sweat it, Mom. We'll get by, and we can probably get into Coquina House in a couple of weeks. Although I don't know what we're going to do when the reno starts."

"We'll delay the renovation," Mom said.

"Not a chance, Beck Foster."

"We might have to anyway with all the trades rebuilding. Oh, the timing of this sucked."

"I think that's the Latin root for the name Dylan," Savannah joked, looking down at the baby. "It means Sucky Timing."

They laughed, but then the door popped open and the discharge nurse came in, her eyes bright and a big smile on her face. "Okay, then, we can get little Dylan checked out, Mrs. Foster."

Savannah just smiled and didn't bother to correct the *Mrs.* It was probably a mistake she'd have to hear her whole life as Dylan's mother. She did make the decision to put Foster as his last name on his birth certificate, but listed Nick as his father.

"Okay," the woman said again, her hands almost trembling when she organized the papers, dropping one. She gave an apologetic smile. "Sorry, it's...always an exciting day when a baby goes home from the ICU."

"I'm sure it is," Savannah said, leaning in for a whiff of His Royal Babyness.

"You can just sign here and here and..." She glanced

over her shoulder toward the door she'd left open, the sound of the nurses' chatter louder than usual this morning. "Initial right here. That means you have a car seat. Do you?" She added a little giggle like a car seat was just the most exciting thing that ever happened to her.

"It's right there." Savannah pointed to the tiny navy carrier.

"Oh, of course, I walked right by it." She chuckled again, nervously shuffling the papers. "I'm all out of sorts today."

"Welcome to my life," Savannah quipped, taking the pen to sign and initial.

"We're ready?" Mom stood up and slid her bag on her shoulder to reach for the baby. "Want me to—"

"Nope." Savannah stood. "Moving is easier now that Mount Baby is getting smaller, but now I have to learn not to drop...anything."

"You won't," Mom assured her.

The nurse walked to the door, then turned before opening it. "You might."

Savannah blinked at her.

"When you see who's here," she added, leaning in with a conspiratorial look from one to the other. "You won't believe this, but Nick Frye is right outside the NICU. Nick Frye! You know, the actor?"

Savannah eased herself back down in the chair, not trusting her legs. "He's...here?" she croaked.

"I know, right?" The nurse did a little shiver with her shoulders. "And he's even better looking in person. All the nurses are absolutely going crazy."

"He's...here?" It was literally all she could say, as breathless as one of those nurses.

"He must know someone who had a baby," the woman said. "He's talking to a group of people and they're all...happy."

She looked at her mother, who just bit her lip and fought some tears.

"Did you see him before you came in here?" Savannah asked.

"No, I didn't. He must have just gotten here." She reached for Savannah. "Would you like to see him?"

"You better hurry before he leaves," the nurse said as she stepped out and held the door for Savannah. "We have no idea what he's doing here, but he could disappear at any moment."

"He could." Savannah stood on slightly shaky legs and smiled at her mother. They just looked at each other, eyes shining and damp, drinking in the moment. "So we better go get a sneak peek of this famous man, huh, Dylan?"

"You okay?" Mom mouthed.

Savannah laughed. "I've never been better. Can you get the carrier and his little bag? I'm going to hold him."

She felt like she was walking through honey and on air at the same time, adjusting the cap on Dylan's head so he looked absolutely perfect...to meet his daddy.

She saw the family first—Ava, Peyton, Josh, Lovely, and Kenny, all talking to...holy wow, did he just get better every time she saw him?

At the sound of her footsteps, Nick turned and his whole face lit up. "Savannah!"

Oh, God. It lit up for *her*? How was that even possible?

"What are you doing here?" she asked as he came closer, arms outstretched.

"I finished early and grabbed a charter." He stopped a foot from her and finally took his gaze off her and let it drop to the baby.

"This is Dylan Foster, your son."

"Dylan." He whispered the name, lifting his hand to touch him, and Savannah saw his fingers were quaking ever so slightly. It almost did her in. "Dylan," he repeated. "You are a handsome little guy."

"Very little," she added. "Really should have cooked a little longer but the storm woke him up."

He looked up from Dylan to her, his eyes wet with tears that just about folded her heart in half.

"We'll grow him. We'll feed him. We'll teach him and love him and..." His voice cracked. "Thank you, Savannah." He folded his arms around her for a gentle hug.

She managed to swallow and not melt into a pool of hormonal mush as everyone else came closer to join in the moment.

"There's a lot of we's in that declaration," she said.

She *had* to know. She couldn't go one more minute without knowing if she'd have to fight him for this child or make some kind of potentially horrible compromise. But now he was born and she had to know.

"What are your plans, Nick?"

He stepped back, including the others in their conversation. "My plans are to take this baby home."

"It's gonna get crowded," Savannah said. "I told you we're all living at Kenny's house."

"I know, so you better pack up, because that's about to change. You're *all* welcome to move in with me. Well, us, since I assume you and Dylan will be there. There's more than enough room for everyone."

Savannah swallowed as emotions rose up and threatened to choke her. "Nick, you can't expect any of us, including Dylan and me, to up and leave Coconut Key and live with you because—"

"Who's leaving Coconut Key?" he asked, looking from her to the others. "I'm staying. I love this place."

"Like I said, Kenny's house—"

"No, the house I just bought on Coconut Key."

"What?" It barely came out as a sound from Savannah's lips. "You bought a house?"

"A big one. With a guest house. A place they call The Haven."

"Oh my God." Mom gasped. "You *bought* The Haven?"

"I did," he said with that darling smile growing into a cocky grin.

"Savannah, that's the house I was telling you about." Her mother could barely get the words out. "The gorgeous one?"

"Is it nice?" Nick asked her. "I haven't actually seen it yet since I came right here, but I've heard there was no damage on that side of the island, because it's on the Gulf. So, we're lucky."

"Lucky? That's putting it mildly," Savannah said. "How did you do this?"

He shrugged, like buying a multi-million-dollar beachfront house was not that big a deal. "When you told me about the storm damage to Coquina House and Lovely's cottage, I had my real estate agent make sure he found a place where everyone could stay comfortably. My only stipulation was that it had to be on Coconut Key."

As the group reacted, the loud cheers and clapping was so loud it made Dylan stir and let out a little sound.

"Did you hear that?" Nick asked excitedly. "Dylan loves the idea."

"You want us all to stay with you?" she asked, still not quite comprehending.

"Whoever needs a...haven." He winked at them and somewhere behind that glass wall, nurses probably fainted.

He reached for the baby. "Can I hold him?"

"Of course."

He tenderly took the baby, a little awkward at first, then he got him in the crook of his arm, glancing over at Ava who was madly taking pictures.

"Hello, little one," he whispered. "What do you think? Can I do this?" he asked Savannah.

"I think you're ..." She just shook her head, speechless. "Unbelievable."

He leaned over and planted a kiss on her hair. "Well, you better start believing me, Savannah."

As they walked slowly out of the hospital, Savannah wiped one more tear of pure happiness. Could she believe him? Could she trust him with her family and her baby and her...heart?

She was about to find out.

Want to know what happens next in Coconut Key?
Click out Book Four...*A Haven in the Keys!* Or sign up for Hope's newsletter to get the latest on new releases, excerpts, and more! Sign up today and you'll also receive a special surprise — the recipe for Jessie's *Anniversary Crab Cakes!* Straight from her kitchen to yours!

Read the entire Coconut Key Series!

A Secret in the Keys – Book 1
A Reunion in the Keys – Book 2
A Season in the Keys – Book 3
A Haven in the Keys – Book 4
A Return to the Keys –Book 5
A Wedding in the Keys – Book 6
A Promise in the Keys - Book 7

ABOUT THE AUTHOR

Hope Holloway is the author of charming, heartwarming women's fiction featuring unforgettable families and friends and the emotional challenges they conquer. After a long career in marketing, she gave up writing ad copy to launch a writing career with her first series, Coconut Key, set on the sun-washed beaches of the Florida Keys.

A mother of two adult children, Hope and her husband of thirty years live in Florida and North Carolina. When not writing, she can be found walking the beach or hiking in the mountains with her two rescue dogs, who beg her to include animals in every book. Visit her site at www.hopeholloway.com.

Made in United States
North Haven, CT
18 February 2022

16253186R00164